Paxton

A ROGUE ENFORCERS NOVEL

DARLENE TALLMAN

Paxton

This is a work of fiction. Names, characters, places, and incidents are either the product of the author's imagination or used fictitiously, and any resemblance to actual persons, living or dead, business establishments, events or locales is entirely coincidental.

Published by: Darlene Tallman

Editors: Mary Kern, Joanne Dearman, Kat Beecham, Melanie Gray, Shannon McFadden, Beth DiLoreto

Cover by Tracie Douglas of Dark Water Covers

Format by Liberty Parker

Model: Christian

Photo by: Eric McKinney / 6:12 Photography

This book is for my dad, Don Tallman, Sr., who believed in me. One of our last conversations, before he passed in 2017, was him telling me that he was proud that I had not only followed my dream of writing, but that I was becoming more known in the community.

Thanks, Dad, for your unwavering love and support. Couldn't have done it without your wisdom, love and protection. I miss you more than words can express!

Donald J. Tallman, Sr.
10/6/41 - 12/31/17

Blurb

Paxton Doherty is a loner, a shifter without a pack, a man without a mate. While his ability wasn't enough to allow him to become a true Enforcer, someone who protects and upholds the shifter laws, he is 'good enough' to be a Rogue Enforcer. Something that the leader, Colton, figured out. Now, he spends his days handling cases in his area and his nights roaming the woods.

He never expects his mate to fall almost literally in his lap. Or the danger that surrounds her that will require not only his skills, but those of several of his teammates in the Rogue Enforcers.

Landry Welch realized early in life that not everyone who smiles at you is your friend. A professional athlete, she's out running one day when she's hit by a car. Tossed into a ditch, broken and critically injured, she realizes that she'll never have what she always dreamed of—someone to love. She knows she's not worth the effort it would take for anyone to break down her walls but wishes someone would take that chance.

Can the Rogue Enforcers deal with this latest threat? Will Paxton convince Landry that she is, indeed, his mate? Will his confession cause her to run?

Prologue

Landry

Another town, another hotel, another race. As I run, I think about the past few years. While in college, I earned a spot on the Olympic team. Competing at such a high level was exhilarating and winning several gold medals was phenomenal. It led to me being approached by several well-known sponsors to compete professionally. Since I grew up in an orphanage, I don't feel like I have an actual home. Living so nomadically is challenging at time but I've made good friends on the circuit, so I often stay with them when I'm in their town. This time, though, I'm in a hotel.

I hear the whine of an engine behind me and move further over onto the shoulder. Glancing to my right, I see a deep ditch and realize if the car keeps coming, I'm going to have to run into it to protect myself.

I feel the impact which sends me flying toward the ditch and my last thought before I lose consciousness is that I never found someone to love or to love me back.

Paxton

THE GROWLING I HEAR IN MY AREA HAS MY HAIR standing on end. This is my territory; I've claimed it when I'm not on the road. No shifter, human or other being should be in this area. I hear the squeal of tires and a feminine yell. My feet react before my mind does. I'm running full speed, my panther taking over as I allow the shift from human to panther to take over. I go to see what's happened with the noises and smells permeating the air around me.

When my nose catches a metallic scent in the air, my pace quickens, and I find a still object lying in the ditch. I stop and crouch down. There's no movement and my heart leaps in my chest when I see auburn strands of hair strewn out across the ground. It's then that my animal senses connect with my human brain. It's a human...female...mine.

Mate.

I've never thought of having a mate, something my mother has lamented over for years. Our last conversation before I moved away from home replays in my head.

"Paxton, there's no reason for you to move. This is your home." Mom sniffles into a Kleenex while watching me load my bags into the bed of my pickup truck.

"Mom, there's only room for one Alpha in a pack and you know it as well as I do." My father became the pack alpha and he and I barely see eye-to-eye on a good day. He's a bit of an overbearing, controlling asshole and the only reason all the responsibility fell to him is because my uncle didn't want it after my granddad passed. He gracefully bowed out and relocated his family halfway across the country, abdicating the proverbial throne to my father.

"Please say you'll visit at least?" she pleads. I feel bad at this moment knowing that if I do visit, they will be spaced out due to the lack of welcoming me back on pride lands from my father. He literally told me I was allowed to visit

my mother once a year, never the family, or members of the pride, just my mother.

"It's going to depend on work, Ma. But you know you'll always be welcome wherever I am." I ended up getting lucky in that respect. Colton Alexander oversees a group of shifters who act as unofficial 'enforcers' of the shifter world and when he heard that I was accepted into Enforcer training but declined, he reached out and offered me a job.

I hear her sigh then feel her arms wrap around me as she hugs me tight. "I know how your father is," she murmurs. "I'm sorry I wasn't able to get us away, but neither he nor his father would let me go and take you with me, so I stayed."

I can't fault her for that, either. My grandfather was only slightly less despicable than my father is, which is one of the reasons why many of my relatives have left. No one needs to be ruled with an iron fist, especially since we tend to be more laid back than many of the other shifters who populate the world now. It didn't matter to him or my father that Ma wasn't his true mate; he wanted her, took her, and has held her hostage from life since then.

"It's okay, Ma. I love you and that'll never change. Just know, if he ever hurts you, I'm coming back to get you myself," I tell her. "Now, I gotta get on the road." Not bringing her with me is hard, but I know if I try to, the pride will come after me on Father's orders.

"Be safe, Paxton. Call me when you can." Saying goodbye is harder than I anticipated it would be. Not a day has gone by that I haven't had her by my side.

"I will, Ma. You stay safe here, okay?" One last kiss on her cheek and I walk away, making sure to look over my shoulder so she knows this isn't as easy on me as I'm making it appear to be. Once I climb into my truck, I take a deep breath, look back at my childhood home, and start the engine.

Looking in the rearview mirror, I blow a kiss at her like I always have since I was a cub. She merely smiles and I pull away worried that I can't take her with me, but I know that her life here will be more manageable without me. Father tends to start arguments, and she tries to play peacemaker.

I force the shift back to human so I can examine the female better. She's unconscious so my naked state shouldn't bother her. Not that I give a flying fuck. Still crouching next to her, my panther whining inside, I gently feel for a pulse, letting out the breath I didn't know I was holding when I feel one. It's faint but steady. Most of the cuts and gashes are superficial, but there are a few that look like they'll need stitches. The deep bruising that already shows has me concerned that she may have internal injuries. Because of that, part of me doesn't want to move her, but I know I can't call for help until I get her back to my place.

Must help her, my panther growls.

"Working on it," I reply.

Hurt bad. Do something!

"I know this! Fuck, give me a second, will ya?" I'm trying to figure out the best way to pick her up and move her without causing more injury when the scent changes.

Must mate her now! She's dying!

Fucking hell. What do I know about having a mate? Will it even take?

No one in my pride was a prime example of how to treat or how to bond with a true mate. The older generation was too scared to reach out to the young and my parents' generation was matched up by the pride alpha, who was my grandfather. He wanted to ensure his pride never left his grounds, and Father continued the tradition his father began. Both of them were and are assholes and they matched people who were of the male's liking, not caring if the female despised the male or not. If someone found their true mate, that mate was escorted out of town; if he or she came back, they were stoned to death. It was unacceptable to bring an outsider in and those born into the pack were forbidden to leave without permission of the Alpha. Luckily for me, my father couldn't get rid of me fast enough. He would've packed my bags and gassed up my truck if I'd allowed him to.

Do it now!

"I'm not sure what to do," I murmur, my eyes roaming over the female.

Before I can say anything else, I feel my fangs elongate and my claws extend as I partially shift. Leaning closer, I scent the fading pulse before sinking my teeth into the space between her shoulder and neck. Almost immediately, I feel the connection as our bond is formed. I couldn't take the time for her to give me permission to change her into a panther and hope that what I'm doing won't have any adverse impact. She may come back to herself and be pissed as hell that she's now a shifter. The good news is, at least she'll be alive to get pissed off and she'll heal quickly once the change takes effect.

"Fuck, I wish I had someone I could call," I say as I pull back. Already, I can feel her pulse getting stronger and some of the more superficial wounds are healing. The scrapes and cuts are knitting together, bruises that had already formed a black and blue hue are changing to a lighter yellow-greenish color. I hope like hell that she's okay with what I did; it's too late now because the bond took and she's starting to change.

Mates can't be separated for long periods of time; we need each other to keep the other sane and physically fit. I begin to go through her pockets, looking for any form of identification or even a phone. All I know about her is that she has long auburn hair, a lithe athletic form, and beautiful bone structure. I know nothing about her eye color or personality, but I already know it doesn't matter. She could be the world's biggest raving bitch and it won't make a damn bit of difference; my panther will see nothing but perfection.

She moans and her eyes begin to flutter. "Shh, you're safe, love." She mumbles something unintelligible, so I reach down and grab her hand. Lacing our fingers together, I hope to give her some comfort with my touch. My panther purrs in contentment. Sometimes, I want to hit him, because now, I've got a mate. One who has no clue what I've just done. The biggest issue, of course, is that we're virtual strangers who must now stay with one another in order not to lose our minds and go feral.

It will be okay. She'll adjust.

"I'm gonna take you home so you can heal in the comfort of our bed, mate." The word *mate* on the tip of my tongue tastes good. Feels good. Knowing I'm now responsible for another's happiness fills my panther with pride and a feeling of contentment and all-out happiness. He's always been a protector, and now, he has someone who will always be there. His own family, my family. A surge of satisfaction sweeps through my mind when he starts chanting about cubs and a forever bond that's unbreakable.

"Cubs! For Christ's sake, panther, take a damn breather already. We don't even know our mate's name," I admonish him.

She's mine, ours, she'll be happy to give me a litter, he states as he prowls restlessly in my mind. *We must claim her, tonight*, he insists.

"Can we explain to her what she is first?"

Why must you make me wait? I've been longing for my life partner for years. Your human side is being ridiculous. He turns his back on me and pouts like a newborn cub.

"She's grown up as a human, panther. She doesn't understand our ways or about who she's to become."

She'll learn. I'm not talking to you until you see things my way.

"Please don't. I've got this." My panther has always been like this; somewhat opinionated and when he doesn't get what he feels is 'his way', he tends to pout. Right now, I need to focus on my new mate, so if he wants to ignore me, I'm perfectly fine with his decision.

When you need me to advise you on mating, don't call. Stubborn son-of-a-bitch. Like I don't know how to insert part A into port B. It's science, I can figure it out without him watching over me.

"Watch out!" she screams. The bluest eyes I've ever seen stare back up at me before closing again.

"Fuck!" She's having a nightmare and I can't stand it. I want to chase all of the bad things away and keep her safe, sane, and protected. I must avenge her and find out who hurt her and dish out retribution. I pick her up bridal style and something drops from her bra. I dip down and pick it up. I have nowhere to tuck it since my clothes are shredded. I place it gently in the crease of her stomach and make my two-mile trek back to the cabin.

Landry

I'M IN AND OUT OF THE BLACKNESS, BUT AS I COME TO, I can feel a washcloth gently swiping across my forehead. The coolness feels good even as my brain wrestles to figure out what is going on and where I am.

"Rest, mate," I hear. There's something about that voice that soothes and calms me. I want to hear more of that deep baritone voice, but the darkness takes root and I can't seem to wake my body. Only my mind is alert, nothing else seems to be working. I allow myself to sleep once again, knowing in my heart that whoever this stranger is, they will protect me.

I come to, off and on. My eyes opened periodically, and I witnessed rays of sunshine in the room earlier, but now it's pitch black outside. I scan the room to see if I can figure out what the hell is going on and where I'm at. I realize immediately I'm not in a hospital. The walls are rough-hewn, like what I've always imagined a hunting lodge or log cabin would have. I'm in an oversized bed that is too big for any human I've ever met. I'm covered with a homemade quilt, it's beautiful, colorful, and extremely comfy. Glancing down, I see I'm wearing a soft t-shirt and a pair of men's basketball shorts instead of the sports bra and running shorts I was wearing when I left the hotel earlier. I have no clue if it's the same day or not and even though this is concerning, I sense that I'm safe. I also feel like I'm not alone in my own body anymore, but maybe I hit my head when I got hit by the car because it feels like something is purring deep inside of me.

"H-hello?" My voice is raspy with disuse. I move to sit up and notice that even though I feel a bit achy, I don't have anything to show for being struck by a car. No bruises, no cuts.

Nothing.

How weird.

I hear someone coming and my eyes focus on the door. When it opens, I feel the breath leave my body as the most beautiful, imposing man I've ever seen walks in, a bowl of something steaming in one hand and a bottle of water in the other.

"Oh good, you're awake," he says, slowly walking toward me.

I don't know who he is, but I hear *mate* and the purring inside intensifies. Shit, I must have hit my head a lot harder than I initially thought I did.

Chapter 1

Landry

You're safe now, Landry. He will protect you. I will protect you. I nearly jump out of my skin as the voice inside of me talks again. I was raised in an orphanage, no one knows of my parentage and I'm beginning to wonder if my mother was a patient in an insane asylum. That would explain the craziness I'm feeling at this very moment.

What the ever-loving hell is going on? Great, now I'm arguing with a voice I hear inside myself. Have I gone cuckoo? Maybe I'm really in a coma or something; this can't be real.

Trust me.

Trust us.

He'll explain it all.

Believe what you already feel in your heart.

"W-who are you?" I ask as he reaches my side.

"Paxton Doherty. We...uh, I found you this morning. Do you remember what happened?" he inquires as he hands me the bowl and opens the bottle of water before placing it on the nightstand next to me.

"I was out running when a car hit me. All I remember after that is flying through the air. How come I don't have any injuries?" I reply.

I intensely watch him as he raises his hand and scrubs it across his face before he runs it through his hair. Even though he's a stranger, I feel a connection of sorts to him, one I can't understand. I feel no fear, just a calm acceptance, even though I'm obviously lying in his bed in clothes that aren't mine.

"Okay, so I need you to keep an open mind." His hesitancy has my nerves ready to flare up in an anxiety attack. I deeply breathe in and out, making sure to count and steady myself before I begin the interrogation of this yummy stranger.

"Keep an open mind about what?"

He sighs and I can see that whatever he's about to say is going to be life-altering. "Alright, let me get this all out before you ask any questions," he replies.

"Humans are unaware of this because of the laws that shifters follow. When you got hit by the car, I heard you yell and ran to see what was going on. I found you lifeless in the ditch near the path you were running. You were severely injured; enough so that you were dying. My panther recognized that you were my mate, so I bonded with you to save your life."

Did he? Did he just say *mate*? This is impossible! I've read paranormal romance before and know that shifters don't exist in the real world. Maybe this man has been injured too?

I know my jaw is wide open. I can't comprehend the words he's just spoken. Shifters? Panthers? Mate? Bonding? I'm not exactly sure where the hell I need to start but first things first, I suppose. "What does bonding mean?" I remember the word from my readings, but I can't seem to remember the definition those authors provided.

"I, uh, I bit you when my panther pointed out that you were my true mate." He has a satisfied smile on his face which causes my anger to rise.

"You *bit* me! Are you insane?" Now my hands are running across my body to see if I can feel anything. My mind starts whirling with thoughts of rabid animals and rabies shots.

"It's up on your shoulder near your neck," he states

helpfully. My hand reaches up and I feel the faintest raising of skin where my shoulder and neck meet. There are two perfectly formed puncture marks and my body begins to vibrate.

"I'm obviously in a coma and having a weird out-of-body dream or some shit," I mutter. My voice is barely over a whisper as I struggle to comprehend what it is he is saying to me. Closing my eyes, I pinch my arm but instantly feel the pain assuring me that I'm not in a sleeping type state.

"No coma, Landry. It's all real."

"You heard me?" Did I say that out loud? I'm usually really good about keeping thoughts to myself. I'm so confused.

"Yeah, that's one of the plus sides of being a panther. Advanced hearing, vision, speed. You'll have all that as well." Good, the speed will come in handy when I go to escape the madness that is this Paxton character. He's got a screw loose somewhere and I'm not a fix-it type girl.

Trust him, that voice inside says. Now it feels as if something is pacing inside of me. I leap out of bed and begin looking around for who was speaking. I know there's someone else there; there has to be.

"A panther? Like a big cat or something?" Lord, I'm trying to wrap my brain around this but it's almost too surreal. I begin pacing the room, giving him a narrow-eyed glare every few seconds.

He grins at me and I see a dimple pop out on his cheek. Looking him up and down, I can see that if shifters were real, he would likely be a cat. He's tall but lithe, and while I can see the muscles in his arms, chest and legs, he's not huge like a bodybuilder. Why am I checking out his stature? I couldn't care less what his physique is. Right?

No. Mate is delicious I hear inside of my head again.

"Stop that!" I holler out.

"What? Stop what? I didn't do anything," he defends.

"Not you," I moan out as I grab my head. "This happened once before. The voice used to talk to me when I was younger. They put me on meds thinking that I had schizophrenia or something. I don't!" I rush out to assure him I'm not going to lose it and need to be medicated or anything. "It's just, why is she back?"

"She? She who? Who's talking to you, who's hurting you?" he roars out.

"Are you sure you're not part lion?" I ask, placing my hands on my hips.

"Nope. No lion here," he spits out as if the thought disgusts him.

"Are you prejudiced against lions?" I inquire.

"Ye-no," he answers confused; as if he's not sure what the politically correct answer should be.

"Um-hmm," I hum.

"Let's get back to this voice." His demanding tone should turn me off, instead it has my panties soaking wet. I sit back on the bed and cross my legs; I'm not sure if it's to alleviate the ache, or if it's because he's sniffing the air.

"When I was a little girl, I would hear a voice inside my head. The caretakers at the orphanage thought I had an imaginary friend at first which is apparently normal for children, but when it contin-ued, they sent me to a doctor. The doctor put me on medicine, and I stopped hearing the voice."

"Are you a shifter?" His question catches me off guard and has me rearing back. Not out of fear, but out of the thought that maybe, just maybe, he's not mental and there are actually shifters who live among us. He begins to pace the room, pulling at his hair, and mumbling about how this shouldn't be happening yet. Yet? What the hell have I gotten myself into?

"I-I don't think so." I try to grab any scrap of infor-mation lodged in my head that was given to me about my birth. Nothing. Zilch. Nada.

"Were your parents shifters?" His question brings me out of my headspace concerning the past and back to the present. He's still pacing and muttering and appears agitated, like something hasn't gone according to plan or something. Pushing that thought aside, I continue. I don't know much, but somehow, I instinctively know that whatever I share is pertinent.

"I grew up in an orphanage. The people there told me that I was found outside a fire department. I have no clue who my parents are," I admit, my head hanging. "They, whoever they were that left me, didn't leave anything on the note except my first name." It's hard to tell a perfect stranger about how unwanted I've been in my life. "Why are you acting like you are? Pacing and shit?"

"Because you're not acting like you're supposed to," he replies. "You usually don't hear your animal until you've gone through your first shift. At least, that's what I've heard from my ma, who told me a story about a human that'd been turned. But since you're apparently already a shifter, I guess that's why you hear her. I don't fucking know and there's no one I know who can help answer that question." That thought seems to upset him further and his eyes begin to glow.

"Well, I sure as hell don't know either, Paxton. To tell you the truth, this is all a bit too much for me."

"You were out running; do you do that regularly?" he questions.

"I've always liked to run, even as a child it always seemed to help clear my head. Right now, I'm training for a marathon."

"Are you fast?" he persists. His eyes are still glowing, just not as bright as before, and I can feel the difference in the energy that's flowing throughout the room. It's almost a tangible thing, but I find I'm not scared.

"I usually win the races in my age bracket. Why?" I feel like I'm being set up to fail where this answer is concerned.

"Because, and this is purely a guess on my part, I think that's how your panther has survived all these years being unable to shift. You had no one to teach and guide you in that part of your being. But I'm here now and you're my mate. I'll teach you."

"Lovely." I know I probably sound a bit sarcastic and snarky, but he's literally turned what I know about myself completely upside down.

He ignores my sass and grinning, asks, "How did you get the last name Welch?" What's with the third degree? I don't know much and am starting to feel hemmed in. I thought I was the one interrogating him, now the tables have turned and I'm not sure how much I like it.

"That was the street I was found on," I tell him. Why am I telling him all of this? It's like I can't help myself and the words are slipping out before I have time to come up with an appropriate answer. "Wait a minute, how do you know my name?"

I hated that doctor, the voice growls, startling me.

"Uh, the voice inside just told me they hated the doctor," I say.

"Sounds like your parents or maybe just one of them was a shifter, but whatever they gave you suppressed that side of you. As for how I know your name, I found your ID wallet." Could this be true? Wait a minute! My wallet was in my bra. I'm mortified, what did he do while I was sleeping?

"Why did it come out now? And...did you *touch* me without my knowledge or approval?" I voice my inner questions out loud.

Because we found our mate, the voice states as if it should be common sense or something.

"She says because we found our mate." I see the gleam in his eyes and my body responds in kind. When I see his nostrils flare, I realize that he can probably smell my arousal and I feel the blush steal over my face. Great, just great. I'm a walking, talking, body of kitty nip.

"You did," he admits. "Well, I found you. To answer your question, it fell out and I picked it up. I didn't go reaching into your clothes. In fact, even though I changed you into something that wasn't torn and ripped, I didn't take any advantages. You weren't awake to ask, and I wasn't leaving my mate in torn, bloody clothing. So, do you have any questions?"

Questions? Jesus, I don't know where to start.

Just ask him, he'll tell you the truth. If he doesn't, you'll be able to tell.

"How? How can I tell?" I ask aloud.

"What do you need to tell?" he returns.

"The voice said I will be able to tell if you don't tell me the truth. Is that true?"

"Your panther is correct. She's a part of you, Landry, and it sounds like she's always been there. Let me ask you this—do your nails grow long and strong? Does your hair always look shiny and healthy? Have you ever instinctively sensed danger looming around you and removed yourself from the situation? How about your sense of smell? Does it seem more pronounced than everyone else's?" His twenty questions make me stop and think.

I start nodding as he continues. "Yes, to all of it.

When I was in college, some of my friends and I went to a party. We were having a good time and then I got that feeling that something wasn't right with one of the drinks that my best friend was given. I wouldn't let her drink it but made her bring it with her and we left. Another friend took it to the chem lab and tested it and it was full of Rohypnol that would've knocked my friend out." She could've been raped or murdered that night if my sense of smell had not been as strong as it is.

"Holy shit, you probably saved her from being assaulted or something." I was just thinking that! It's like we're connected; using one brain as one. United, bonded...wow! How freaky is this?

"Yeah. After that, I went with them to all the parties and 'sniffed' their drinks so they'd know if it was okay to drink or not."

"What about you?"

"Drinking has never been a big thing for me. I will say that I can outdrink anyone." Yeah, like that's something to be proud of!

"Most shifters aren't able to get drunk. It's our high metabolism. Speaking of which, I need to feed you."

"I could eat," I admit when my stomach starts to growl. He grins at me and holds his hand out. Instinctively, as if we've done it for years, I lace my fingers in his and stand up. I can feel the heat from his body and hear the purring inside grow louder as a different scent crosses my nose. When I hear a growling rumble come from Paxton, I look up and notice his nostrils are flared.

"You need to stop, Landry."

"Stop what?" I ask. I mean all I'm doing is walking beside him. I can't help that he's hot as hell and I'm all kinds of attracted, can I?

"Even though you've healed from the accident, we can't act on the desire we both obviously feel."

I raise my eyebrow at his words. "How do you know?" I suspect he smells it, but I want it confirmed, so I ask.

"Because I can smell it and I know you can smell mine as well. It's making my panther crazy; he wants me to fully mate with you right now."

I stop moving, his words resonating in my head. The purring inside intensifies and is now so loud I feel as if I have a jet engine inside.

Mate delicious. We must have him.

"We don't know each other!"

"We're mates; we've got the rest of our lives to get to know one another," he replies.

Paxton

THE LOOK SHE GIVES ME AFTER I SAY THAT HAS ME biting back a grin. "Landry, nothing's gonna happen until you say so, okay?" I feel my panther swipe at my insides and I stifle a grunt; he can be a prick at times, and apparently, he's not feeling my declaration.

"Um, okay," she whispers. I can smell her desire and see the physical evidence as her nipples are so hard, they're protruding through the t-shirt I put on her like she doesn't have a bra on. "I don't know what to do with all of this, Paxton. I mean, up until a few minutes ago, I thought that shifters were just something I enjoyed reading about, y'know?"

"It's okay. I honestly never thought I'd have a mate, let alone my true mate. So, we'll figure this out together, okay? I just need to give you a heads-up, though. We can't be separated for too long or we'll get physically ill. If we go beyond a certain timeframe, we'll become feral."

"Well, I don't want that, so I guess you're stuck with me," she teases.

Our mate is funny. I like her.

"Not thinking that's gonna be a hardship, Landry," I tell her as I mentally agree with my panther. She is funny and it seems like she rolls with the punches pretty well. Although – there's a hint of sadness around her eyes that bothers me and even though she's teasing and laughing, it's as if she's still on guard. My goal, however, is to break that wall down. She's going to be my mate in every way, shape, and form.

Chapter 2

Paxton

We walk into the kitchen and I lead her to the table. It's not like the cabin is huge, not by a longshot. Two bedrooms, one bathroom, a kitchen, a living room. And the second bedroom currently houses all my workout equipment and computer shit, so Landry will have to share my bed. Not that you'll ever hear me complaining about this problematic situation, hers not mine.

This makes me happy, my panther says.

"Have a seat and I'll fix something for us," I say. I hate letting her hand go and it dawns on me that even though we haven't fully bonded and won't until we have sex, we're already connected in a way that I don't ever want to lose.

"So, do we eat different things?" she asks. I stop and think about her question; we eat normal food when in our human form, but we have an accelerated metabolism, so our caloric intake is higher than normal.

"Not really. We can eat more because we've got a high metabolism, something you probably have noticed previously, even with your panther suppressed. When we're in our cat form, we'll eat anything we catch raw, of course, but at home, it's cooked." I see the face she makes when I say 'raw' and can't help but laugh. "Baby, it won't feel unnatural when we're hunting, trust me, okay?"

She is handling this well. I think we should have the mating talk. I want cubs.

I sigh because now that we have a mate, my panther is going to be insistent that we push for cubs and that's something I want to make sure that Landry is one hundred percent on board with before I try to make it a reality.

"Why are you sighing? This is all too much for you, isn't it? I should probably go," she says, standing from the chair she's been sitting in while I've been cooking.

"What? No, my panther is being a bit pushy about something and I don't know how else to tell him that he has to be patient."

"What's he pushing you about?" She's genuinely curious so I give her an honest answer.

"He wants cubs," I tell her.

"He wants the Cubs to do what?" It dawns on me that she thinks I'm talking about the baseball team and I chuckle.

"Not the Chicago Cubs, baby. My panther wants *us* to have cubs. You know, babies?"

"What?" Her voice rises three octaves at my words and there's a look of horror and fear on her face.

I crouch in front of her and take her hands in mine. "Landry, why are you scared about having cubs? Is it because of your own past?"

She keeps her eyes averted but replies, "I'm still trying to wrap my head around the fact that I'm a shifter, we're now mates, and my life has changed, and your panther is ready to hop to the next phase. Talk about a wham-bam situation. Plus, and this is important, I don't know my parentage. What if I'm not fully panther but mixed with something else? Wouldn't that screw things up?"

"I don't scent anything else but panther on you, Landry, but we won't know for sure until you shift for the first time. As for the other, my panther can just be patient. We've waited all our lives for you so we can wait until you're ready." I feel my panther roam restlessly at my words before he finally flops down with a huffing sound.

Fine. We will wait, but we want it noted that we will do everything to make it happen sooner rather than later.

Oh jeez, this means I need to be on top of things; otherwise, my panther will try to manipulate the situation so that he gets what he wants.

"How long before I shift?" she asks, breaking me free from my musings.

"No clue, since your animal was suppressed for so long. I need to figure out who I can call to see if they can help us out." I wonder if Colton knows? Maybe Maverick? Or Alarik? Guess I can start with Colton and work my way through the others. Someone's bound to know.

"So, are you going to find someone to call?" she inquires.

"Yeah, I'll do it later after we eat."

"Oh, okay. I guess that works."

"Is it okay if I get cleaned up?" she asks while we eat. "I feel grimy." I grimace because I was more concerned with getting her bloody clothing off than making sure she was shiny and clean.

"Yeah, sorry I didn't think about that," I reply. "We need to go over to the hotel too and get your things. Wait, maybe I should handle that since we don't know who ran you off the road and whether or not it was deliberate."

"I don't exactly have anything to wear, so maybe you should be the one to go. Did you happen to find my room key?"

"It fell out the same time your phone did so it's probably on the nightstand next to the bed," I tell her, picking up our empty plates. "I'll run to the hotel and clear out your stuff and drive your car back, then you'll have clean clothes to change into after you shower."

"Okay. I was supposed to check out tomorrow anyhow, so one day early won't matter. Do you really think it was done deliberately?" she asks.

Mate in danger.

My panther may be ignoring me, but he's prowling restlessly after her comment, which tells me there's more to her accident than we currently know.

"I'm not really sure, Landry. My panther is reacting strangely, but it could be because we're mates and since he's also pissed off at me, I won't get a straight answer."

She starts giggling and is soon laughing so hard that tears are streaming down her face. I wait for her to calm enough to speak, anxious to hear what is so damn funny. "Y-y-you say that so nonchalantly, as if someone hearing it wouldn't find it odd that you've got a voice inside of you talking. Hell, I've got one too." More laughter follows and soon, I'm joining her because it's true.

Non-shifters definitely wouldn't understand and would lock all of us up if they heard how we talk about our animals. "Guess we need to be mindful when we're in mixed company, huh?" I ask.

"Probably so, although it's been so many years since I've heard mine, I'm sure I'll be the one blurting shit out."

"Well, the good news is, we tend to be a bit solitary, so if you promise to keep me in check, I'll do the same for you," I tell her. "Let me go grab the key and I want you to program my number in your phone." She nods and I leave her to grab both her phone and the hotel key, as well as my own phone.

"It shouldn't take you too long. I didn't really unpack anything."

"Did you leave your purse and all that in the room?" This bothers me because anyone could have gone in there while she's been gone.

"I did, but I have the 'Do Not Disturb' sign on the door, so hopefully, no one has gone inside since I've been here," she replies.

"I'll be back as quick as I can," I say before leaning down and kissing her forehead.

Why are we waiting for cubs again?

"Trust me, buddy, I hear you on that one," I mutter as I walk out the door. Just that simple touch has my body on fire, something I know she's not ready for yet.

Landry

"I MAY AS WELL EXPLORE A BIT WHILE HE'S GONE," I murmur to myself. He cleaned the kitchen up already, but I go over the counters, anyway. Then I see the notepad on the refrigerator and realize it's a grocery list, so I grab it and start checking the cupboards for anything he might need. Once that's done, I go through the fridge and freezer, and add the meats that I notice he seems to have a lot of onto the list.

Now bored, I head into the bedroom and strip the bed since I know I didn't have a shower. Even though Paxton cleaned me up, the thought of climbing into the bed after a shower has me cringing. "I'll just throw this in and see if he has another set somewhere," I say out loud.

Mate very handsome.

"Yes, yes he is," I reply. I can still feel the touch of his lips across my forehead, almost like a brand, and despite knowing him a handful of hours, I want to throw caution to the wind and feel him thrusting inside of me.

I approve of this idea.

"Of course, you do, you and his animal are out of control," I state.

Not yet we aren't.

I roll my eyes at her words. "Stop being so damn dramatic. It's not like you've been around all these years pining away for a mate. You just showed back up, remember?"

Not my fault. The witch did it to protect us.

"Witch? What the hell are you talking about?" My mind is spinning with this revelation and I wish Paxton was here. Witches exist? Paxton told me about shifters and them coming in all animal forms, but he never mentioned other supernatural beings existed. Does that mean Spiderman, Hulk, and Thor exist as well? Are there superheroes living amongst us? And if that's true, do vampires, ghouls, ghosts, trolls and giants exist? Vampires, damnit, I never considered their existence. Makes me wonder if there are any good ones out there, or should I start wearing turtlenecks everywhere I go. Maybe I'll make myself a garlic necklace to ensure my blood's safety.

The witch knew you weren't safe if others knew about me. She put a spell to bind me that would stay in place until your true mate came along. I've always been here, watching and waiting.

"Why wasn't I safe? Do you know who my parents are? Are they still alive? Why didn't they keep me? I don't understand!" I feel like my world is spinning on its axis and not planning on slowing down anytime soon. Should I be taking notes?

Yes, to the supernatural creatures but no to the superheroes. They're made up, probably by people who have sensed shifters and can't figure out a way to explain them.

All of this is too much for me right now and I collapse onto the couch once I've started the laundry.

Talk to Paxton, he'll help you understand everything. Besides, mate is yummy.

"I don't want to talk to you anymore," I moan out. "You're making my head hurt." I need to search through Paxton's medicine cabinet and see if he has any pain relievers. Do panthers tend to get migraines? If not, maybe I have a brain aneurysm, either that or

I've fallen into the abyss and am living in an alternate universe.

You're in danger, Landry. That accident was deliberate. And we don't get sick or carry diseases.

Wait, what? "What do you mean, I'm in danger? From who? I don't have any enemies!" Maybe it's my panther who needs psychological help. She's seeing things that aren't in existence.

From the past, Landry. They've found you.

"Oh, for the love of potato salad! Who the hell has found me?" Great, now I'm arguing with my panther. This should guarantee me a one-way trip to the psycho ward.

You're not crazy. Paxton and his friends will help protect you. Mate will protect you with his life.

What if his friends don't like me and don't want to protect me?

What's not to like? We're pretty awesome, actually, and your mate already finds you delicious, funny, and irre- sistible. They will always want to protect you because of their association with him. She's so sure of herself, of us, she sits back in my mind and is licking her paw. As if I want to see her bathing herself. She needs to close her damn legs, that should be a private thing.

"Get out of my head!" Now my thoughts are no longer my own. "And stop showing me your nether regions! A girl should keep some things to herself." Indecent I tell you!

No, they're not. And I watch you when you bathe, so what's the difference? We have the same parts, I just have more fur.

"Stop watching me when I bathe! And no, we don't. I only have two nipples!"

The more nipples we have the more cubs we can birth.

"No you didn't! As a human I only have two nipples and I'd prefer having only one child at a time, thank you very much." My irritation with her is growing stronger with every second that passes. She's a smartass little bitch.

I'm very smart. Trust me, Landry. I've kept you alive all these years.

"Um, just saying, but you were suppressed until a short time ago so how do you figure you kept me alive?"

Every time you sensed danger, you ran, right? Who do you think let you know that danger was near? It was me. Now she's preening and patting herself on the shoulder. I don't know if I should envision myself strangling her or ignore her. Either works for me right about now.

"So, you're saying that even though you weren't

allowed to shift, you were still helping me? Then who am I in danger from?"

The past.

"Well, that answers so much. Thanks for the enlightenment. Catch ya later, you damn she-bitch!"

Chapter 3

Paxton

I finally make it to the hotel, grateful for my excess speed that helped me get here in a matter of minutes by foot. I take the room key from my pocket and head to Landry's room. Once inside, I glance around but don't see anything out of place and I don't smell anything either. Good. I head into the bathroom where I find her travel bag. Quickly grabbing the items in the shower, I shove it all in and go back into the room. She wasn't lying; her suitcase is still closed but up on the second bed. I open it up and put her travel bag inside and see her purse. Dammit, I hate the thought of going into her purse, but I need her car keys. The sense of urgency I feel being away from her continues to increase and hasn't been helped with my panther's insistent growling.

"I'm hurrying up, asshole," I grumble. I feel him swipe my insides and grunt. "Keep it up and it'll take me longer to get back home." *Home.* Already it sounds better knowing that she's there waiting on me.

Mate in danger. Hurry!

I look around the room one more time before I lay the card key down on the table and pick up her suitcase. My panther's anxiety has me hurrying out of the room and out to the parking lot. I don't know how he knows she's in danger because that part of the bond generally doesn't happen until we've fully mated, but at this point, I don't care. She and I have a connection that may be more emotional at this point and if that's what has him cluing in to the fact that something's up, I'll listen. I click the fob and thankfully, the car nearest me lights up.

It's about time you listened to me.

"Listen here, I do when it's important." He still has a lot to learn; not everything is about him and his wants. There's a fine line between desire and being realistic with a situation.

Hurry.

"Will you stop? I can't afford to break the speed limit, dammit. She'll be fine until we get there. Remember, I've got a helluva security system and I set it before I left." At least that's what my intuition is yelling at me. He's a bit overdramatic at times, I'm praying this is one of them.

Doesn't matter. Need to put my eyes on her. And I'm not overdramatic.

"Oh, Jesus fucking Christ. She's not going to vaporize! We're only a few minutes from the house so get yourself under control." While scolding him, my heart is rapidly beating inside of my chest and at this point I'm not sure who I'm trying so hard to convince; him or me.

Yourself. I know she's in danger even if you won't believe me. Drive faster.

I'm grateful that I'm near the house because I decide to err on the side of caution and hit the gas. As I pull into my driveway, I look around but don't see anything to warrant my panther's sense of urgency.

She needs you. She needs us.

I grab her suitcase and purse, lock up her car and jog up the steps of the porch. Quickly unlocking the door, I key in the alarm code and once I've shut the door, lock it behind me. "Landry?" I yell out. Fucking panther has me acting like some wet- behind-the-ears girl or some shit.

"Back here," she replies. I carry her stuff back to the bedroom to see her remaking the bed.

"What are you doing?" I ask, setting her stuff down. Maybe he was so out of sorts because we were away from her, but now that we're home, he's backed off some.

"Since I slept on the bed when I was dirty, I pulled those sheets off and put them in the wash. I found another set and figured I'd make the bed while you were gone. I also made a grocery list."

Mate is handy to have around, see?

"Um, you said you wanted to grab a shower. I'll place the food order online and we'll get it delivered."

"It's a lot, Paxton," she states, a small grin on her face. "I added some things that I like to eat and drink."

"As you should since you're my mate," I tell her. "Fresh towels are in the cupboard in the bathroom. I'll be out in the living room waiting on you."

She nods and walks over to her suitcase. When I see some of the lacy things inside, I groan and quickly walk out of the bedroom, adjusting myself. This being patient shit is for the birds. It's never been a quality of mine and I don't see it becoming one in my near future.

Landry

MATE WANTS US.

"Trust me, I know, I can smell it," I mumble as I grab clean clothes and my travel bag and head to the bathroom. As sensitive as my hearing has gotten, I know his is as well and I don't want to answer any questions about what I meant, so I'm hoping he's otherwise occupied and didn't hear me.

Everything she said earlier is still swirling around in my head as I get the temperature on the shower set while I strip out of the clothes he put me in after cleaning me up. Looking in the mirror, I'm still surprised that I have no marks left on me; maybe this quick healing shit has something going after all. I don't even ache and I know, based on how fast I was running and roughly how quickly the car was moving that I was flung a significant distance. Enough of one that I should have had broken bones or possibly been dead.

Mate saved us.

Yes, yes, he did. On that I agree fully, even if everything I ever knew about myself is now part of some strange world.

You're still the same person. You just know about me now is all.

"Not sure that's such a good thing since you've been talking about witches, being in danger, and the fact that you want cubs," I state, leaning my head back under the shower head. The cabin isn't particularly big, but Paxton went all out in the shower. It's big enough for two people at least, and he has several shower heads that are positioned throughout the stall, allowing me to stay warm while I wash my hair.

Big enough for two panthers.

"Shut up! I can't even hear myself think right now!" I feel my panther flounce to the back of my mind, grumbling to herself as she turns her back on me.

I'm not gonna complain about her ignoring me. I need some peace and quiet from the growly bitch. All I wanna do is scrub myself clean and rinse her from my mind. Since she decided to come out and make herself known, I've had to hear her complain and bitch about everything. Sometimes it's as if a little old lady is residing in my mind.

I'm not old! And I'm not a growly bitch.

See! She has to have the last say about everything.

"Just give me some quiet time while I shower. I need a break from your outburst and whining."

Panthers don't whine.

"You could've fooled me."

You need to understand that I'm a part of you. Not a separate entity. I can hear your every thought, feel everything that you do; I will protect us at all costs.

"Joy," I mumble.

You'll learn to deal and love me.

"If you say so." I throw a mental block up, hoping it will help, but doubting it will do so. She's persistent, and oblivious to my needs.

I'VE JUST FINISHED SCRUBBING MY HAIR WHEN I PULL out my razor. I hear a growl in the depths of my mind. "What's wrong now?"

Hair on legs is sexy.

"No. No it's most definitely not." Ignoring her, I grab my shaving cream and lather up my right leg. As I perform the motions I've done a thousand times, my mind wanders to Paxton. Based on what I've scented, he desires me as much as I do him. This could prove to be interesting, to say the least.

My leg now done, I go to rinse it only to see hair again. What the hell? "Knock it off," I tell my panther.

No need to shave. Mate won't care.

"Well, I happen to care, dammit!" Once again, I shave my right leg and stare in astonishment as after each swipe of the razor, the hair grows right back. "You need to stop this, right this instant!"

No, you need to stop.

"Oh my God, I can see this is going to be a challenge," I mutter, as one more time, I lather and shave my right leg. When the hair grows back for the third time, I throw my hands up and yell, "Paxton!" I don't know if I will be able to handle this panther living inside of me. Something needs to give; she needs to chill or I need to find a way to let her know who's really in charge.

Paxton

I HEAR LANDRY YELL FROM THE BATHROOM AND RUN TO see if she's okay. Maybe my panther was correct and she's still in danger, except he said nothing. When I open the door expecting to see her standing there, I'm met with her panther, lounging in the shower, soaking wet.

Mate is stunning.

I look at her panther, who is lying there, her facial expression one of satisfaction, as if she beat Landry at something. First things first, I need to get her dried off. "Landry?" I question. Her head lifts and I'm met with stunning blue eyes. A flick of her ears tells me she heard me, but she turns her head. "Don't ignore me, Miss Fuzzy Butt. You need to come out of there so I can get you dried off."

She does have a fuzzy butt; this is a good name.

Oh, for fuck's sake. I can feel my panther's excitement as I move toward the shower so I can turn it off. Once that's done, I grab one of my overly large, fluffy towels, and sit on the bathroom floor. "Come here, Landry, and let me help you get dry." I hear her panther make a chuffing sound before she stands, stretches then leisurely strolls over to me. Her moves are graceful, and I picture a time when we can both be in animal form. I can't wait to teach her to hunt, play, and embrace the panther residing within her.

Can't wait. Let's do it now.

"No, we're not doing that now. My first time with her has to be in human form and you know it," I mumble. Landry finally reaches me and flops down, placing her head on my thigh. I feel myself reacting to her nearness, as well as the desire that I scent permeating from her. It's like a perfume that my animal can't resist. It makes her irresistible to him and he goes into a frenzy whenever she's near. It's how mates are meant to be. There is no one for us who can attract us like the one specifically made to be ours.

Mate wants us, see?

"Landry, why did you shift?" I murmur as I work to dry her off. Unlike a lot of cats, panthers don't mind water that much which is why I redid the bathroom so the stall was so large. I wanted to be able to laze underneath the water without going to the creek that's out in the woods, especially during the winter.

A low purr starts to rumble from her chest as she lifts her head to look at me. Right now, I wish we were fully bonded because then I could communicate with her through our bonding link, but until she shifts back to her human form, I'm stuck wondering, what happened?

"Guess I'll have to wait in order to get my question answered." I finish drying her and stand. "It's been a rather eventful day. How about we relax for a bit before dinner?" She nods her head and follows me to my bedroom where she proceeds to jump on the bed and curl up. I slip off my shoes and crawl in next to her. When she rolls over to where she has her head and upper torso across my body, I feel a sense of pure satisfaction and contentment roll through me.

Mate is perfection.

The purring from within, as well as Landry's panther purring soon lulls me to sleep.

Chapter 4

Esmeralda

I smile and wave as my last clients pull out of my driveway. Once they're gone, I close and lock the front door, then head into the kitchen. It's time for some tea and meditation; Mrs. Clemmons and her sister always take a lot out of me when I have to do a reading for them.

Once my tea is ready, I carry my cup to my sitting room and sit in my comfortable reclining chair. The crystals, stones, potions, precious gems and oils I have placed in there are specifically to provide me with a calm, serene environment. Sighing, I think about my day and how I'm not really using the magick that I was born into. Four generations of witches have come before me, yet I'm the only one left thanks to the witch hunters who eradicated most of my coven. My mother and grandmother hid me with their magical cloaks, making sure I wouldn't be seen, even if the worst happened and they perished.

I was hoping to one day have descendants to pass my teachings to, but I haven't found my soulmate as of yet. But a lady can always hope. I'm old in human years, but when it comes to the paranormal realm, I'm considered a young child. I'm over a hundred years old, but I look like a woman who's still in her early twenties. My lineage is old, we're not someone you want to cross or go up against; we're considered the most powerful of our kind, and live long, fruitful lives. But yet, I find myself in hiding, giving readings to the townsfolk, predicting futures and contacting deceased loved ones.

Years ago, my best friend, who was a panther, passed away. The day her precious baby was born, I made a promise to protect her young with my last dying breath. In order to do that, I had to go into hiding and become known as the crazy old lady. My best friend was a black panther who fell in love with a human male. Their love was something everlasting and even death can't sever their bond. Jazzy, my bestie, died protecting her baby and mate. Her pride hadn't had a female birth in over twenty years, so when Landry was born, they came for her. Claws extended, battle cries could be heard far and wide. They were determined to eradicate her parents and steal Landry away so that when she matured, they could mate her with the Alpha.

I used the magical cloak and covered Landry so they couldn't see her and escaped with the clothes on my back. In order to protect her, I put a binding spell on her panther to suppress it, then utilized the 'Safe Haven' law and dropped her off at a fire station. But I've never lost sight of where she was; I imbued a crystal with her essence so that I could watch over her. I also managed to get something of the Alpha's and did the same so I could be sure he never found her.

Thinking about Landry has me glancing over to the table where her crystal sits. When I see it glowing, I smile because that means she's finally found her mate. My good mood evaporates when I see that the Alpha's stone is also glowing; that means that he has located Landry.

I must go to her and help protect her like I promised Jazzy. Standing, I take care of my now-empty cup, then head to my computer to check my calendar. Seeing no upcoming appointments, I quickly do a finder spell and locate Landry. Then I throw a bump in the Alpha's road, I send him in the opposite direction; making him believe she's left. I want to give myself some time to make it to her, explain things to her, and help her fight to preserve her life and that of her mate.

My curiosity gets the best of me, so I pull out my crystal ball and check in on her. When I see who her mate is, I smile. He's a Rogue Enforcer, he has allies, and he and his friend, Maverick—the hybrid—will make a difference in the path of the paranormal road we were headed down. It was a dark path that now has a ray of light shining through. I clap my hands in glee, the future doesn't look so gloom and doom.

One suitcase and one booked flight later, I'm on my way.

Chapter 5

Paxton

Iwake up with a warm, naked female in my arms instead of the panther, causing my body to heat up and react.

She's here. You're here. We should mate.

I shake my head at my panther's words, even though there's nothing more that I'd love to do than sink inside her delectable body. "Soon," I whisper, my hand lightly stroking her shoulder and upper arm. She's so warm and soft that I feel my restraint being tested, so I ease away from her and slip out of the bed.

Stupid idiot. She's our mate.

I ignore his grumbling and head to the bathroom

to clean the mess we left earlier. Once that's done, I grab my phone and call Colton to see if he knows how we can find out information on Landry's parentage. I know it's a longshot, but she was rather adamant about no babies until she knew, and I know my panther won't rest until he's impregnated her.

"What's going on, Pax?" Colton asks when he finally picks up the phone.

"Got a possible situation and I'm not sure which direction I need to look," I admit.

"Give me the rundown and we'll see if we can figure something out," he replies. I fill him in on how Landry was struck by a car, how I turned her once I realized she was my mate, and how it's apparent she was already a shifter, only she doesn't know her parentage.

"The only one who I think could possibly help is Maverick," I state. "I haven't reached out to him yet because I wanted to get your take on things."

"He'll probably be your best shot since he has that ability," Colton says. "Since you called, want to fill you in on some chatter. There's a pack out north looking for a female shifter. She's supposed to be their alpha's mate or some shit. No clue how true the rumor is, but is there any way that this Landry could be who they're looking for?"

I close my eyes at his words. Something deep inside tells me that her 'accident' was intentional. When my panther growls, I realize that he's on the same page as me. Landry has a target on her back and it's up to me—to us—to protect her while eliminating the threat. "I don't know, Colton, but my animal is nearly shredding my insides so I'm going to agree with your assessment."

"Keep her safe. I'll keep nosing around to see what else I can find out. You let me know if any of us need to come out and help you."

"Will do. Thanks, man."

"No problem. Keep your mate safe."

I hang up and head into the kitchen to fix breakfast.

Landry

I WAKE UP TO THE SMELL OF BACON AND SMILE WHEN I realize that I'm back to myself. My *human* self that is; hairy legs and all. Rolling out of bed, I glance down and grimace when I see that I'm naked, then I pray that Paxton didn't notice. Huh, he's a guy and they always notice that kind of thing. Shrugging, I go over to my bag and grab some clothes for the day before heading into the bathroom.

Once I've handled my morning routine, I head into the kitchen and straight for the refrigerator. "Score!" I mutter when I see my favorite diet drink. Grabbing a bottle, I search through the cabinets and find a stainless-steel mug with a top. I fill it with ice, pour my drink over it, then take a long drink. "Ahh." I'm so lost in my thoughts that when I feel a hand on my shoulder, I jump and scream.

"Sorry, baby, I thought you knew I was in here," Paxton says, pulling me into a hug. I relent a little because being in his arms makes me feel safe and secure, something I've never really had.

"Needed caffeine," I reply, taking another drink. "I woke up smelling bacon, but I don't see any," I muse, glancing around the kitchen.

"Got it in the oven to keep warm," he states, pulling away from me. "Go have a seat and I'll get it." I nod and head over to the table, continuing to suck down my drink like it's water. "Here's another one of those," he says, placing another bottle in front of me. "Seems you're working to re-caffeinate."

I start giggling because he's telling the truth. "I am. It's probably my one vice, for lack of a better word. I love the smell of coffee, but don't like the taste, so this is the compromise I made myself."

He hands me a plate and sits down so we're almost touching. "Did you sleep okay?" he asks while peppering his eggs.

I feel my face heat up when I remember that I woke up completely naked. "Uh, yeah, I did. How about you?"

He grins and winks before replying, "Any time I wake up with a beautiful, naked woman in my arms is a good day." I feel something like jealousy take root at his words and the low growl that forces its way through my lips has him staring at me.

"So that's happened frequently, huh?"

"No, in fact it's never happened. That's why it's such a good day," he replies. "To have it be my mate? Fucking awesome."

I shake my head at his words because this whole mate thing still kind of stresses me out. "I have so many questions, Paxton. I don't even know where to begin." The rapid thoughts and questions in my head have my head pounding and my palms sweating.

"Let's begin with the first one that pops into your head." His calm demeanor helps me focus.

"Well." I clear my throat, "I suppose the first one would be, how do I control she-bitch taking over my body? I know I'm supposed to be sharing, but sometimes I'd like to stay human. And how can I keep her from growing my leg hairs back?" I lift up my pants and show him the fuzzy black hair. "I shaved three times, Paxton. *Three*!" I see a gleam in his eyes when he looks at my legs, but other than the purring I hear inside, he doesn't say anything.

Mate likes hairy legs. I told you so.

He begins chuckling. He goes to say something a few times, opening and closing his mouth before bursting out into a full-blown laughing fit. "Your panther's a controlling one...huh?" he eventually asks.

"I don't think controlling is a strong enough word for what she is," I answer, blowing the steam coming off of my plate. "I have all sorts of names for her, but she doesn't seem to care for any of them."

"Well, if you're calling her a she-bitch, I'm sure she's having a reaction to the reference." He places a napkin over his mouth to hide his smirk, only he's not as sly about it as he thinks he is.

"What else do you call her?" he asks, but this time, I see the gleam in his eyes. He's curious, but also, I seem to be his comedy relief. It makes me wanna smack him.

"I'm a lady. It would be scandalous if I said those words out loud to a man." Choke on that, pussy cat!

Shit, now I'm rhyming. What has this creature done to me?

I am better than a domestic house cat. I run faster, am more intelligent, and you actually like that I'm here now and you can hear me again.

Fat chance, sister! I feel like I'm going to come apart at the seams and I've got Paxton acting like it's funny as hell, and my panther attempting to run everything. I can't deal with this right now.

"Where are you going?" he questions as I jump up from the table. I don't answer; I head to the bedroom where I grab my running clothes before I walk into the bathroom. A good, long run always clears my mind.

Oh, I love it when we run!

"Shut.The.Fuck.Up!" I grumble under my breath. I'm done with snarky, bitchy comments from my panther, done with the man who won't answer my questions. Just plain done. Wisely, she doesn't say anything, allowing me to change before I head out the door. Right now, I don't even care that I look like damn Big Foot with my hairy legs.

"Landry! It's not safe," Paxton says, standing on the porch.

"I'll be fine. Remember, I can run faster than most everything," I reply. "I need to think and you're not helping by not answering my questions."

"Let me go with you at least."

"Defeats the purpose of me being *alone*," I state.

I see his shoulders drop and feel a slight bit of remorse, but I shrug it off. Maybe when I get back, he'll answer my damn questions.

Chapter 6

Paxton

ate mad at you. "No shit, Sherlock. What was your first clue?" I grumble out as I go back into the cabin.

Need to fix this.

"Again, I definitely get that, just don't know how." I mean, it's not like I've been in a lot of relationships before. In fact, other than finding the occasional release from a one-night stand, I've never even had a fucking girlfriend. Now, I have a mate, one I have no clue what to do with and my panther's advice is not helping.

Google is your friend.

"What the fuck? What do you mean by that?"

Go research. Find out how to fix this so we can mate and have cubs.

"Right now, she doesn't even want me around," I mutter as I clean up the kitchen. My panther's right, though; I do need to fix this somehow. It's just that her reaction was so funny, I couldn't help but laugh.

You need to teach her.

"Yes, oh wise one, I'll get right on that." He acts like he's fucking Yoda or something.

She doesn't know our ways.

"I realize that." Then it hits me between the eyes; she's been thrust into something that she only ever thought was fiction, only to find out it's now her reality.

Finally, you're listening to me.

"Yeah, whatever. I'm busy right now." Think, Paxton, think. How can I show her that everything's going to be okay?

Maverick! His gift, it will help her to see that everything she's feeling, the fears she's holding onto, will all be worth it in the end if she bides her time and rides this wild time out with me. I snap my fingers and grab my phone. It's time to pull my friend from his self-proclaimed reclusive ways and make him join the land of the living.

"Lo." He answers the phone in his standard way.

"Need your help. Need you here."

"On my way. Where ya at?" No questions asked. I say I need him, and he's willing to leave the darkness and come help me out.

"Home."

"See ya soon." He hangs up and I know shortly, Landry will be introduced to a living-*breathing*, hybrid. Half vamp and half wolf. Good times ahead.

Landry

As my feet pound along the roadway, my mind drifts back to how Paxton reacted earlier. Away from him, his presence, I realize that I might have overreacted just a little.

You think?

Ah, there she is - Queen Snarky! I snicker at my latest name for her, but when she starts to purr, I realize that I might have found something she and I can both live with. "You like that one?" I ask. My breaths are coming out in short pants; I didn't take the time I normally do to warm up and I'm paying for it right now.

It's the best of all of them. So far.

"Did I overreact?" I question.

Yes.

Well, that was short and succinct. Now, how do I fix this mess?

Mate with him. That will fix everything.

"Sex isn't the be-all and end-all of life," I mutter. Not that I'm massively experienced or anything. A few meaningless flings when I was in college just to see what all the fuss was about left me feeling cheap.

It will be with our mate. Trust me.

"Why the hell do you think it'll be different? And why the hell would I trust a word you have to say. I now know you have no sense of style...hairy legs my ass." She has my curiosity aroused now, but I don't want to seem overeager to hear her responses.

Because he's our mate. It's his responsibility to bring us pleasure, keep us safe, and give us cubs. I would roll my eyes again, but at this point in time, I fear they'll stay stuck at the back of my skull.

"There you go with the cubs bullshit again. I'm not ready to have kids, and I only want one at a time."

We'll see. You'll change your mind.

"That's it, I'm done." I slow myself until I come to a

clearing. My brain is overloaded, and I just want to bash something. Seeing a tree branch on the ground, I grab it and start swinging it against the tree, while yelling and screaming. In the back of my mind, I realize I look like a two-year-old having a tantrum, but right now, I don't give that first fuck.

"What on earth could that tree have ever done to deserve that treatment?" a female voice asks from behind me.

My eyes widen in shock at the thought of getting snuck up on without hearing or smelling something foreign in the air. Screeching, I spin around, brandishing the branch like a weapon. The petite woman standing in front of me with a burgundy cloak wrapped around her doesn't say anything, she just stares. "W-who the hell are you?" I sputter out while my breathing settles down some.

"Esmerelda, child. I saw you were in danger and came right away," she replies. She *saw* I was in danger? The fuck is she talking about? I haven't left these woods since Paxton rescued me. Great, another person in my life that needs to visit the psycho doctor. What in the ever-loving fuck is going on in my life? I slump to the ground, my head in my hands as her words wash over me. I mean, I don't generally curse as a rule, but these past few days have shown me that tossing out a 'fuck' here and there never hurt anyone, and it conveys a ton of emotion!

She's here to help us.

Oh, now Queen Snarky decides to show up!

She's been protecting us since you were born. Trust her.

Ah, the mystery deepens. Looking at her, I ask, "How do you know I'm in danger? Who are you? I mean, besides your name."

"I need to speak with you and your mate at the same time, child. Come, time's a-wasting, and we don't have much of that to begin with." She motions to me, almost imperiously, and I stand to walk over to her. Once I'm close enough, she touches my wrist and before I can utter a word, we're on the porch at the cabin. I stumble from the suddenness of the warped speed of travel and my stomach is turning. I don't think I'll ever get used to the way my new life is turning out to be. This is a lot for one person to deal with in such a short time span.

I can't wrap my brain around anything at this point and simply follow her inside. My sense of urgency has me calling out, "Paxton? We, uh, we have a guest who needs to talk to us both." I'm still eyeing the stranger, waiting for the next shoe to drop in the adventure I call life.

He walks into the room and comes right to me,

pulling me into his arms. Suddenly, things feel right again, now that he has me wrapped up in safety. "Who are you?" he asks, his voice gruff and growly. Glancing up, I see his eyes are glowing and realize that his panther is close to the surface. His face begins to change, then as quickly as I blink my eyes, it's back to normal again.

"Can we sit down to talk?" she responds, moving toward the couch while taking her cloak off. Go ahead, make yourself at home. She gives me a sharp look before saying, "Child, you have no idea what home really means."

Paxton doesn't say anything, he simply picks me up bridal style, so I lay my head on his shoulder. Being here like this, secure in his arms, gives me a sense of calmness, and I feel like I'm home when I'm snuggled close to him. He then walks us over to his chair where he sits down and pulls me against his chest. Once he's assured of my safety, he looks at Esmerelda and says, "Start talking."

My heart pitter-patters at the fierceness in his tone. My panther purrs in my head and I mimic her causing Esmerelda to smile at me with mirth in her eyes. I narrow my eyes in her direction and she barks out a singular laugh.

Our mate will protect us. Always.

I feel an answering rumble against my back and look up to see him staring at me. His eyes are like a window to his inner thoughts and I feel myself responding to what I see; desire, lust, passion, and something that I can't quite define...but the intent in his eyes has me doing a full-body shiver in response. I snuggle closer to him and allow myself to relax when it fully hits home that he will protect me at all costs because I'm his mate. Not just his mate though, it's something stronger, more passionate, more protective and it makes me want to climb him like a monkey in a tree—right here and right now.

"Lady, I'm losing my patience here. Either start talking or get the fuck out of my house." His voice has gotten raspier and I know without looking that his panther is so close that I'm surprised to see hands, not paws wrapped around me.

Our mate is getting pissed off and it's turning me on. For once, I'm in agreement with Queen Snarky, the damn she-bitch, so I say nothing. I feel a huff, almost like a giggle and have to hold my own back because it's obvious, at least to me, that we're facing a shitstorm of epic proportions.

Chapter 7

Esmerelda

I look at the couple in front of me and smile. Landry's mate is beyond what I ever expected, and I know that if Jazzy were still alive, she'd be thrilled. First, however, I need to make sure that they realize the extreme danger that she's in so they can take the appropriate measures to ensure she stays safe.

"What do you know of your past?" I question, looking at Landry.

"Nothing. Well, other than I was left at a fire department. I grew up in an orphanage until I was eighteen. Been on my own ever since," she replies.

Taking a deep breath, I say, "I knew your parents.

Your mother was my best friend in the world, even though we're different."

"What do you mean by different?" Paxton asks, glaring at me.

"Her mother was a panther and I'm a witch." No sense in beating around the bush and I've got too much to do to ensure her safety. "Your father was human, but your mother fell in love anyway, saying he was her mate. She never turned him though, something I wish she had done because maybe the outcome would've been different. When she became pregnant, the alpha in her pack decided that he wanted the child. She enlisted my help and after their deaths, I got you to safety. In order to make sure you remained that way, I put a binding spell on your panther, then dropped you off at the fire station. I've been watching both you and the alpha all these years to ensure you stayed out of harm's way."

"Why does he want Landry?" Paxton asks.

"Because Jazzy was special. She had some unique abilities that the alpha was hoping would pass to her child. He plans to mate with Landry which is why it's imperative that the two of you don't wait much longer to consummate your mate bond."

I watch the couple as my words sink in and see her sink further into his arms. I know that I need to explain their mate bond further but can see how over-whelmed Landry is becoming. "W-what kind of abili-ties did my mother have?" Landry's voice is small, unlike the confident, strong woman I know she really is and if I had a heart, it would break seeing her sound so defeated.

"She was telekinetic," I reply. "The alpha was hoping that she passed that on to you because with his own abilities, a child created by the two of you would be very powerful and ensure his reign."

"She's not going anywhere," Paxton growls out. "She's mine."

His claiming of me to another person causes my panties to dampen in desire. I don't know how much longer I can hold my panther and human self off from claiming our mate. Something I haven't shared with these two love-birds is that I can read minds and hear what Landry's thinking loud and clear. I suspect their mating is going to happen sooner than she thinks.

"No, she's not. Do you know if you have that or not?" I ask Landry. "I know you just broke the binding spell, so it's possible that it hasn't revealed itself to you yet." *I haven't really experienced anything strange outside of the normal having an extra person reside within me and her magically growing leg hair back. If that's an ability, I've got that one aced!* It takes everything I have to hold off from laughing at her inner dialogue. It's more information than her godmother needs to know. Usually, the fact that I can read minds is a gift I treasure, right now though, I wish I had some plugs to ignore what's running through her and Paxton's minds. Some information can be too much information...I normally can block them, but I need to know what they're thinking since they don't know me, nor trust me. My need for damage control and instant expected faith is necessary as of now.

"Queen Snarky hasn't told me if we can move stuff with our minds yet. Wait, does that mean I can be like that sister on *Charmed*?"

"Focus, Landry. I need you to focus right now. Wait, you call your panther Queen Snarky?" No wonder her beast is restless and conflicted. They need to become one, it's the only way she'll come out on top.

"Look what she did to me!" Landry exclaims, showing me her legs. "She wouldn't let me shave my legs; she said hairy legs are sexy and my mate would love them." I cover my mouth to keep myself from laughing out loud at the expression on her face and the venom in her words.

I may not be a shifter with enhanced hearing, but I hear Paxton whisper, "I'll show you how sexy I think you are later." Even my jaded heart speeds up a bit and

I feel a blush coming on. I haven't blushed in at least fifty years; this man in front of me definitely has 'it' in spades.

"Seems as if she's trying to mark her territory and show you who the boss is," I remark, hiding my grin at her disgruntled look. "Paxton will teach you how to control her, but that's not our priority right now."

"Where's the danger coming from? I mean, obviously from that alpha, but has he come himself or sent some of his pack? If so, how many? I may need to call in some of my fellow Rogues," Paxton inquires. I see he's a man on a mission and nod to myself. He'll keep her safe. And someday, I'll hopefully have their children to be a pseudo-grandmother to. Everyone needs a fairy godmother, right? I can try to turn some pumpkins into a coach and mice into horses. And, I know I can magically make her a pair of see-through slippers...I'll add some sparkle to them for her. Maybe the night they have their mating ceremony I can make it special for them.

"The alpha found Landry and has likely sent one of his men to capture her. However, he may be close by," I state. I don't miss the look they share with one another and am instantly on alert. "Tell me what's happened," I demand.

Paxton tells me of their initial meeting, and I

realize that the alpha's man is closer than I assumed when I sent him on a wild goose chase. "I suspect if you hadn't come along and rescued her, he would have come back and kidnapped her." Her mother and father would be turning over in their graves if they realized how much danger their daughter was in. I did everything I could to protect her, but it seems it wasn't enough.

"As a matter of fact, I did hear a car pass by, but I was too focused on Landry," he replies.

"Do you think they'll try again?" Landry inquires.

"Until the two of you have consummated your bond, you're in danger, yes," I reply. "I can place a protection spell around your property, Paxton, but that'll only go so far." I'm suddenly weary; the events of the past day have piled on and I realize I need to sleep. "Do you have somewhere I can rest for a bit?" I ask.

"As a matter of fact, because I get visitors from time to time, I built a tiny cabin out back. It's got several bedrooms since I never know if I'll have more than one person showing up." I nod at his words. I know his cabin isn't big enough for more than them and then I grin wondering if he'll build onto it once they have children. It's the perfect location for a pair of panthers —heavily wooded—and I know there's a stream or river out back because I saw evidence of it when we were standing on the porch.

"That will be perfect. Let me grab my crystals then take care of the protection spell before I rest." I snap my fingers and my bag appears, eliciting a gasp from Landry. "Once you get used to traveling like this, you'll never go back," I quip. I head into the kitchen to get some of the items I'll need. "Oh, and can I get some hair from each of you?" I may as well toss in a lust spell for the two of them to speed this mating shit along.

Chapter 8

Landry

While Paxton shows Esmerelda where she'll be staying, I putter around the cabin. He's definitely a neat freak because there's nothing for me to do. Hell, he's already folded the laundry *and* put it away. Not sure I can live like that, because I tend to leave it in the dryer until it's needed.

I decide to take a bath to see if I can relax a little bit.

Mate likes hairy legs.

"Can I please, at least right now, have clean-shaven legs?" I ask as I head into the bathroom. It truly is a work of art, with a separate tub that's big enough for two. I feel her huff as she plops down.

If you must. He won't care.

"I know he won't, I saw the look in his eyes and smelled his desire. But I care and you and I are one, so shouldn't you be on my side here?" I realize I'm pleading with her, but dammit, something has got to give. My whole world has turned upside down and I need to retain some control.

Fine. Well, I know what I mean when I say that word; just hope she doesn't feel that way.

"Thank you," I whisper before slipping into the tub. While she and I were arguing, I tossed in some fragrant bath salts and heave a sigh of relief as the warm water envelopes me. "Damn, this feels good, doesn't it?" I ask.

I enjoy water.

"Yeah, I figured as much seeing as you turned me yesterday." I realize how funny it is to be talking to myself and start giggling. "It wasn't humorous when it happened, but now it's hysterical to think about what you did!" She makes a noise that sounds suspiciously like a giggle and that sets me off again. "Maybe this shifter thing won't be so bad."

You'll enjoy the stamina.

"Look, Queen Snarky, I can't deny that he makes

me want to do things, but the hype is more than the reality. At least in my experience."

Because it wasn't your mate.

"You sound like a broken record sometimes, you know that?" I question as I start shaving my legs. I don't worry about my hoo-ha, opting to trim it up instead. I've never understood that craze because it seems to be almost more trouble than it's worth. It takes a lot of time and maintenance and I barely like picking up my razor in the first place. If long hair on my legs didn't itch and hurt so bad when I wore pants, I'd say fuck it and go all natural.

So that's why you like to keep it short?

"Yeah, it drives me crazy in human form. Can we compromise? A little bit, at least?"

Fine, you can shave, but I reserve the right to let it grow back at any time.

I roll my eyes. "Okay, drama mama, if you must. Now, I have a mate to find. Do you think he'll want me?"

Mate wants us.

"Thanks for your vote of confidence." I finish up my task and get out of the tub, grabbing a huge fluffy towel to dry off. Once finished, I rinse the tub, then work on smoothing lotion into my skin before I brush my hair and teeth. I slip into my nightgown and head toward the bedroom. It may be late afternoon, but I'm exhausted. As much as I want to find Paxton, right now, a short nap is in order.

I WAKE UP ALL WARM AND COZY. TURNING MY HEAD slightly, I see Paxton's head on my pillow, his arms and legs wrapped around me. When I feel him harden against my ass, I can't help but wiggle. "Don't start something you're not going to finish," he rasps in my ear. "Because I've got a hair trigger where you're concerned at this point, and it won't take much to make me lose control."

Rolling over so I'm facing him, I run my hand down his cheek. I love how smooth his face normally is but seeing him with a five-o'clock shadow has me clenching my legs. "Who says I don't want to finish this?" My desire for him is off the charts and I want to explore the feeling. "We're mates, right?" His eyes start glowing again and I snuggle closer, wanting to feel his muscles against my softness.

"We are, but you've had a lot of information tossed at you in a short time."

"So?" I counter, reaching my hand between us to grab the hard dick that's been pulsing against my stomach. "Seems like it doesn't really matter in the big picture." I start stroking his length, silently wondering how I'm going to make it work. He's far more endowed than the few men I have been with in the past.

He'll fit, trust me.

Great, now Queen Snarky has decided to weigh in on the current situation. "Kiss me, Paxton, please?"

His head lowers, and I feel his lips lightly touch mine. The spark that ignites at his touch has me pulling his head closer before my fingers dive into his hair. As the kiss deepens, I hear myself moan. His hands are doing their own exploring and I feel a callused hand brush over my breast. "God, Landry, you're so soft and warm."

"Mm-hmm," I reply, too lost in his kiss and touch to formulate real words. "Touch me, Paxton." I don't know why my desires for him have ramped up like they have, but becoming one with this man has become my primary focus in life. The thought doesn't seem to scare me as much as it did when he first told me about who and what I am. Then, I was ready to run for the hills. Now, I want to make sure the world knows he belongs to me and *only* me.

"Whatever my mate wants," he murmurs, before lowering his head to nuzzle my neck where our bond mark resides. His hands continue to roam my body, sparks of need ignite within, then suddenly, my nightgown is pulled over my head. "Ah, much better," he states, licking his bottom lip as he continues looking at my naked body. I feel a flush start to go up and down my frame, from head to toe, and know that I'm turning red. "Nothing to be ashamed of, Landry, your body is one that men have fought wars over." Before I can respond, he lowers his head and takes a nipple in his mouth. The sensations that wash over me at the touch have me nearly growling with need.

He continues his ministrations, and I find my legs moving restlessly in an attempt to soothe the ache. "I'll take care of you," he whispers. "Patience, baby."

"God, Paxton, I don't know how much more I can stand," I reply. Okay, I may have whined a bit, but I'll never admit to that...the confession will never be heard out loud, not from my lips anyway.

He lifts his head and grins at me, his eyes full of passionate desire. "Trust me, Landry, I'm in the same boat. There is so much I want to do to you, with you, and I sure as hell don't want our first time to be quick." Quick works for me, but I'm at his mercy and will let him lead me down the path of *purr*-dom.

"Quick or slow, it doesn't matter at this point," I murmur. I can feel my juices running down my thighs and I know I'm more than primed for him. "Please? We can do slow later, because there are things I want to do to you as well." I'm willing to put my hands together and beg him with my eyes and mouth as long as he gets the damn show on the road.

He raises himself over me, settling his hips to where they rest between my thighs. "You're so fucking responsive, Landry."

Hmmm...he's so yummy, and his voice is always rough, growly, raspy and all man.

She-bitch, go away. This is my time with Paxton. You'll have plenty of opportunities with his other half. For now, I'm gonna try that blocking thing he told me about so I can ignore your interfering ass.

I prefer Queen Snarky, if you must call me something. Fine, go have your fun. Just remember, you've both got stamina.

Mind your own beeswax and move on! In my head, she turns around, sticks her ass up in the air and tosses a 'fuck you' look my way over her shoulder before she completely turns the other way and ignores me.

"Only with you, Paxton. Never been like this before," I admit as the head of his cock bumps against my clit. I've never orgasmed during sex before, but the shiver that just went through me tells me that things are about to change. Reaching my hand down, I guide him to my entrance and then hold my breath as he slowly enters me. The slight stretch from his huge invasion tells me that I'll be feeling him for a long time to come. I'll remember him for days on end...I hope and pray that I'm not too sore to do this again. I'm already addicted to him and have a hard time being out of his presence for long periods of time. It makes me feel weak, insecure, and vulnerable.

"God, Landry," he groans out once he's fully seated inside me. I can feel his breath on my neck and his balls resting on my ass. He's absolutely perfect for me in every way that's humanly and pantherly possible. Before I get a chance to respond to his words, he slowly trails his hand down my thigh, once it gravitates behind my knee, pulling one of my legs wider, stretching me as far as he can, which allows him to be seated deeper inside of me. He slowly starts thrusting his hips backward and forward, then does something where his hips circle and my eyes cross. I gradually wrap my other leg around his waist trying to make sure he doesn't escape and go anywhere. My hands grip his biceps while my nails dig deep into his skin. The sight of him, face intent, hair flowing around his head and down around his shoulders, has my pussy clenching. "You keep that up and this'll be over before we get good and started, baby," he hisses out.

"Don't stop, Paxton!" He nods and lowers his head to my breasts once again.

"Not planning to, until we're both as limp as a noodle." His thrusts get harder and more erratic, then they become faster paced and I find myself spiraling toward something I've only ever personally experienced by my own hand. I reach down and circle my clit with the tip of my finger, my eyes begin rolling back in my head. The increased sensation where we're joined has me picturing him pounding into me over and over again for the rest of our lives...very long lives from what I've managed to learn...Go me! I'm one lucky little she-bitch.

"Paxton!" I scream as my orgasm rolls over me. I swear it's like an out-of-body experience, complete with stars and quite possibly, the face of God. He thrusts a few more times before he throws his head back, his eyes closing in passion as he begins calling out my name. He briefly slumps over, both of us finding it hard to maintain our body weight. As promised, we're both limp and our limbs are unmanageable. He leans down, pecks me on the forehead then rolls to his side, so that he doesn't end up crushing me. I have no words, my mind is jumbled, scrambled, elusive and has forgotten to be cognizant. I numbly, lovingly, continue to stroke his sweat-slickened body while the remnants of my orgasm ebb and flow.

Is it too soon to announce that I love this man? Would he run for the hills if I were to share this emotion overwhelming me with him? God I hope not, because sooner or later, the words are gonna slip from my mouth. Whether it's purposely or not remains to be seen.

Paxton

HOLY FUCKING HELL! NEVER IN ALL MY LIFE HAS anything felt this powerful and I find myself wondering if it has to do with the fact she's my mate. I smooth her hair back and kiss her temple, watching her beautiful face as she works to control her breathing. Not that mine is much better. I feel like I single-handedly ran up Mount Everest.

I think that will give us cubs.

I can't help it, I start to chuckle. "What's so funny?" she asks, turning her head slightly to face me.

"My panther apparently has a one-track mind

where you and I are concerned," I admit, still laughing.

"Let me guess, cubs?" she responds.

"Uh, yeah. Only, as much as I'm going to want them, I'd like it to just be us for a bit. At least until we know all the danger has passed, you know?"

She snuggles closer before replying, "I agree. And just for the record? I'm really glad you found me and saved me."

"Anything for you, my mate." I only wish I'd been able to find her before those who are after her did. I'd have made sure that they hadn't been able to track her or locate her. My panther growls with fury when I think of the danger she's potentially in.

HOURS HAVE PASSED AND IN BETWEEN BOUTS OF lovemaking, we've napped, showered, gotten dirty again, and eaten. I know there's a threat against her, but right now, being with her like this is where I'm supposed to be.

I'll be damned if the past comes back to haunt her. I'll pull all of my markers, make promises to whoever I need to, to ensure her safety. I'll never let anyone...*anything*, ever invade our lives and take her away from me. She's mine and I'm a protective son of a bitch when it comes to those I deem as mine. If anyone fits that particular category, it's her. It'll always be her.

I'll kill, maim and gnaw on the bones of anyone who poses a threat to her life. My panther agrees with me and begins to rub his nose against my leg and purrs intently.

I love our mate. Me too, but I'm going to wait to tell her because the last thing I want is her freaking out. She still lives in the human world, her brain hasn't wrapped around the way a shifter's life works. She doesn't get that for us, love is instantaneous. We know upon meeting our mate that they are our world, our love is magical and unbreakable.

We'll wait...she'll accept it. She's smart.

Now you want to be patient? Where is that kind of thinking when cubs enter your mind?

Cubs need to happen. She won't leave once we place our seed in her womb.

Motherfucker, you are crazy as fuck.

Whatever.

Esmerelda

I smile when I see the newest crystal begin glowing. Now that the two of them have fully mated, I'll be able to protect them better. At least until we can get the threat eliminated. Grabbing my bag, I hum as I work up my latest spell.

When I have all of my ingredients, a vision hits me. *I see the hybrid, he's on his way and he will look into her mind and bring back all of her memories.* This couldn't have worked out better if I'd planned it myself. A smile graces my face as I continue to mix and chant.

Things are going to get messy before the storm has passed. But the end...yeah, that looks bright. But first, we have to have the good times prevail and triumph over evil.

Paxton and Landry must conceive and break the chain. Their kids, and a few of the others, they will change the world and we will no longer have to be in hiding. This is a day I've waited for and can't wait to see come to fruition.

Chapter 9

Paxton

Early the next morning, before the sun has fully risen, I hear my phone ringing. When I remember that I left it in the living room, I groan because the last thing I want to do is disentangle myself from my mate. When it stops and then starts up again, I realize that whoever is calling needs to speak with me. If it's ringing back to back, it's important...could be an emergency. Groaning again, I ease out of the bed, grabbing a pair of sweatpants to slip on, then I proceed to go and search for my phone. Damn cold floors! I don't have many rugs in the house, so the draft in the house is always cool in the mornings. It doesn't seem to matter what season we're in, it's always fucking cold on my damn feet.

"This better be important," I growl out in greeting, not even checking the caller ID to see who's calling before stabbing that damn green button.

"Well, hello to you too," Colton replies. "Figured I'd call for an update. See if you figured out what the hell was going on." I sigh when it hits me that I never called him with the newly discovered information. He's gonna get a kick out of a witch being involved. Colton loves everything supernatural. It intrigues him and he believes in protecting lives of all of us...if it's at all feasible.

"Shit, man, there's so much, I'm not sure where to turn, to be honest. Maverick's on his way, and yesterday, some witch named Esmerelda showed up. Seems she knew Landry's parents and is the one who suppressed her panther. The Alpha of her mother's pack is the one after her and it appears that the little accident she had the other day was their attempt to snag my mate." I can feel the fury rising when I think about what was planned for Landry. If it takes my last breath, they won't touch her. No fucking way.

"Do you need more of us? I can put a call out," Colton states.

"Naw, think I've got it for now. Like I said, Maverick's on his way and the witch said she was putting some sort of protection spell on the two of us."

"You know the sooner you two mate, the more protection she'll have," he says.

"Already been taken care of." There's no fucking way I'm giving him any kind of details; that's between me and my mate.

"Good to hear." I can tell he's grinning and wish I could reach through the phone to hit him. "You've been waiting a long time for your mate." His words take the wind out of my sails a bit; he's a supportive fucker and has all of our best interests at heart.

"Yeah, I have. Never expected to find her like I did, but she's mine and protected." My fear of mating wrong was from lack of my upbringing, but as my friends have slowly started settling down throughout the years, it put a damper on my mood. I have always felt the loss of love and attention in my life; my mother was as loving as she could be, but I needed more. Still do and am happy with the mate the fates have chosen for me. She's perfect in absolutely every single way that counts.

"Never expected anything less. Gonna let you go. Keep me posted." I hate saying goodbye to my friend, but my mind is scattered and the only thoughts going through my mind are...protect, mate and produce.

Your plan is solid.

This time, I'm the one who says 'whatever' as I roll my eyes. Fucking animals!

"Thanks, Colton." Once I disconnect the call, I head out onto the porch so I can shift for a run. I know Esmerelda has put a protection spell on us, but I'll feel better if I put my own eyes on my property. Quickly shifting, I head out to run around the perimeter. Even with my speed, it still takes nearly thirty minutes, but I'm satisfied that nothing that's not supposed to be on my land is there.

I RETURN TO THE HOUSE AND HEAD INTO THE BEDROOM to grab a shower. I'm sure my woman would love to smell my natural scent, but the human in me knows that the human in her would sneer at my sweaty essence. Seeing Landry awake, I end up taking a detour to the bed and ask, "Want to join me? We can get dirty again before we get clean." Memories of last night are now playing on repeat in my mind. It was so much fun getting her dirty only to put my hands and mouth on her to get her sparkling clean. I can't wait until the danger has passed and we can shift and fuck. The thought has me groaning, because as a panther, she was quite fetching.

Her grin causes me to lean down to kiss her, uncaring about my state of undress. "Yeah, help me up, big guy, and we'll go and see what we can get into." I scoop her up and carry her into the bathroom. Once I have the right temperature of water, I carry her straight into the shower. Sitting her down on the bench, I admire her body as the water slickens her skin. My eyes shift and I start getting our shower supplies in order. While not paying attention to her, she squats down on her knees and sneak attacks me. I gasp out when a warm mouth surrounds my dick, I widen my stance and take her face in my hands. My thumbs begin to stroke her cheeks as they hollow out to take me deeper down her throat. When she goes and swallows, my knees almost buckle. Luckily, I'm able to keep my stance and begin running my hands through her brown locks.

"Feels amazing, Landry," I groan out, whispering words of encouragement and all but begging her to never stop. My knees once again nearly give out as she swipes her tongue across the head. It's a feeling of euphoria that I want to experience every day for the rest of my life. She hums in agreement and I feel a shudder run through my body. Her hand steadily strokes what she isn't able to fit into her mouth, causing my balls to draw up, when it hits me that this will be over all too soon if she keeps it up.

She makes a sound of disapproval as I pull her off my dick, but I smile, pick her up, and then I bend her over the bench. Her pussy opens up like a flower in this position and my dick weeps with want. Fucking perfect height for what I have planned for her. My fingers slip between her folds and my heart rapidly beats when I find her wet and ready for my intrusion. Knowing that she's patiently waiting for me, my chest puffs out with pride, when I realize that she reciprocates my desires. "Feel good, baby?" I whisper as I nip at her back, my fingers thrusting in and out of her. I'm not a small man by any means, and I know I need to get her ready for me, so I begin scissoring my fingers. She starts pushing her hips back, causing my digits to invade her deeper than I had initially planned.

Made for us.

I know. I sorta said it first. Go away.

Not fair. I want to enjoy our mate too. You've become a stingy bastard.

Fuck off. This is my time, you'll have playtime...sometime.

Not good enough.

Well, it'll have to be. Go away, or I'll make sure to

have some commentary ready for you to hear when it's your turn.

Ass.

Never claimed to be anything but. Now leave.

Fine. I wait a minute, but when he gives no further words, I concentrate back on the waiting woman in my life. The very needy, vibrant, intelligent, sexy as fuck woman.

"The only thing that would feel better is if you'd stop playing around and fuck me," she replies. I remove my fingers, smack her ass, and impale myself in the slick heat of her pussy. When I'm surrounded by her warmth, my initial reaction is to thrust inside of her, coat her womb with my seed and procreate. Fucking panther, he's always in my head...even when he's not.

"You sure are sassy this morning. This what you wanted, Landry? Me fucking your tight pussy?" I've got one hand on her hip and the other is lightly stroking and teasing her clit. My eyes are zeroed in on the place where she's stretched wide to accommodate my girth. It causes me to grow harder and longer.

"God, yes," she moans before swiveling her hips. I see stars and realize I'm about to lose control. Her head goes back, and her long locks of hair fall down her arched spine. It's wet and heavy, making me want to reach out and grab it between my fingers and pull her head back and lay a claiming kiss on her lips.

"Do that again," I instruct, thrusting harder. I gather some of her wetness and start working her clit in earnest. When I feel her pussy tighten further around my dick, I increase the pressure and am rewarded with her scream of pleasure. I don't wait; I can't, and my orgasm rushes over me. "Fuck!" I yell, as I gentle my thrusts so that we can both ride out the aftershocks of our release.

"Holy shit, Paxton. Never knew it could be like this, not at all!" I'm both proud and horrified. I'm happy I've made her feel like no other ever has, but I'm pissed and sick to my stomach when I think of another man's hands on her.

You weren't exactly a monk before she came along. Don't be a hypocrite.

Shut. It.

"Only with you, baby." I'm not blowing smoke up her ass; I've honestly never experienced what she and I have. But I'm not going to share that with her, I don't want her feeling an ounce of disappointment knowing another woman has felt me inside of her. It's not fair to her, and would do nothing for me if she thinks of it. Well, that is unless she lets me claim her again and again to where she forgets why she was upset in the first place. Food for thought if I ever piss her off.

You've learned well. We may have to be sneaky with her so we don't upset her and knowing you, this will require a lot of work on my part.

Does he really think the sun sets on his ass? Clean up *my* mess? No, it'll be more like me cleaning up after his fuck ups. The fucking asshole always puts me in the middle of his tricks. He's been known to be a prankster with my friends, then I have to go in and make excuses for his immature ass. If he keeps it up, I may put a moratorium on any cubs for the next ten years. Minimum.

You wouldn't dare, you want them as well.

Yeah, I may want them, but I want to further solidify my bond with Landry. I wonder how soon is too soon to tell her that now that we've bonded, we can communicate without actually speaking. It's rather automatic, but initially, she's going to have to concentrate. I open my mouth to say something, only to realize that this information could possibly toss her over the proverbial ledge. No, I'll wait. I notice that we're both back to breathing normally, so I pull her into my arms and start gently washing her body. "I love touching you," I say as my hands stroke down her sides. "Doesn't matter that I just had you, I want you again already." Her smile lets me know that she's feeling the same. "How about we wait until later? Maverick should be here at any time and I want to see how Esmerelda did overnight."

"Okay. We've got the rest of our lives."

Our very long lives.

For once, I agree with the beast that resides within. I quickly get us washed up and out of the shower, but I can't resist smacking her ass as we head into the bedroom to get dressed.

I leave Landry in the kitchen fixing breakfast and head out the back to see how our resident witch is faring. Knocking on the door, I wait for her to arrive and have to hold my grin when I see that she's wearing a long, flowing dress-like thing. "Young man, I'll have you know this is extremely comfortable," she says as she opens the door.

At her words, I start laughing. "Wanted to check on you and see if you needed anything."

"No, I'm fine as of right now. I do have a few spells I'm currently working on, did you need something?" she asks.

"Landry is making breakfast, so I thought I'd check to see if you were hungry. Also, another Rogue

Enforcer is on his way, so you'll be sharing the space."

"As long as they have their own bed, and aren't scared of a little hocus pocus, I think we'll be just fine," she replies. "I'll eat before I get started because sometimes, I forget when I'm in the middle of things. This old mind ain't what it used to be." Her smirk lets me know she's full of herself today. The interactions I've had with her here and there are easing my nerves where she's concerned. One thing I have figured out is that she's a sneaky little thing.

I nod at her even though I don't have the first clue about magical things. "Well, I'm sure it's important to keep your strength up." Her smirk becomes a full-blown smile and I can't help but wonder how old she is exactly. She looks to be in her thirties, but in order to be around when Landry was born, she had to have been in her late twenties or early thirties at least. Right? I reach up to scratch my head while thinking on this. I swear she hears my thoughts when she starts crowing, her laughter just what you'd imagine a witch's to be like. It's kinda creepy but enthralling at the same time.

She will help fix things.

"Well, we'll see you in a few." She nods as I head back to the house. Hard to believe that just a few days ago, I was living a solitary, lonely life. Now I have a mate, one who is in danger, for now, and my property is unilaterally filling up with other supernatural beings. I smile when I think of what Landry's reaction will be to Maverick. He's definitely different; a hybrid, something that's not usual in my world. As a matter of fact, it's unheard of, and he's a tracked man, always in hiding unless Colton, or one of us, needs him for a job. His life and safety depend on how well he blends into his surroundings. Half wolf, half vampire, he has powers that defy logic. He's also somewhat of a loner, like myself, which is probably why we get along so damn well. He's probably the best friend I have, and vice versa. At least that's what he told me one night after we downed a few gallons of moonshine. We don't get drunk like humans do, but we can get a good buzz going if we continually drink...and that night we did. I walk into the kitchen to see Landry humming to herself as she pulls something out of the oven. "Whatever that is, it smells fucking amazing," I tell her as I reach her. Pulling her close, I lean in and kiss her until we're both breathless and our chests are heaving. The things this woman does to me wow me each time we're in each other's proximity.

"You had the fixings for blueberry muffins. I made those, then I ended up cutting some fresh fruit I found in the fridge's bin. If you want me to fix eggs or anything, I can do that as well," she replies. Once she mentions fresh fruit, all I can imagine is laying her out as a buffet and eating all of the pieces off of her flesh. I lean down and adjust myself before I look back up at her, giving her all of my attention.

"What you mentioned sounds great to me. I'm going to grab the yogurt; I like mixing it with my fruit."

"What kind is it? I kind of like Greek yogurt myself," she admits.

"As a matter of fact, that's the only kind I'll buy," I reply.

See, mate was made for us.

I ignore that prickly fucker and keep myself on task.

We finally get everything to the table and sit down to eat when I hear a knock at the front door. Must be Maverick. I get up to answer it, saying, "That's another friend that I think can help us."

"Okay. Um, I'll get another plate. Will he want coffee?"

"Probably. He can get it himself, though, because he's been here before." Plus, I'll never share this with her, but he doesn't like anyone touching his plates or cups. He gets their life story with just one touch and he has a hard time throughout the rest of the day.

"Paxton! I don't want him to think I'm a shitty mate!" she hisses at me. I start laughing and am still doing so when I open the front door.

"Mav! You made fantastic time. Come on in," I say as I open the door wider.

"You said you needed me so I came as fast as I could," he replies as he follows me in once he closes the door. "So, where's your mate? And I sense we're not alone here either." His eyes narrow as he begins searching for the interloper. He doesn't like many people, and it takes a bit for him to warm up to the ones he does...but he's trying. It's better than how he used to be like before he joined the Rogue Enforcers. At least he doesn't answer the phone when I call with a grunt anymore, I'd say that's progress.

"She's in the kitchen. We just started eating breakfast, so you're welcome to join us," I reply. "And you're correct. We have the witch who saved Landry here as well." He looks at me and his eyes glow red. He bares his teeth for a second then reins them in. He shakes his head and looks up to the ceiling. Once he has himself under control again, he looks at me and it's like Jekyll and Hyde, he's a completely different person. It's freaky as fuck the way he does that.

"Well, that's definitely interesting," he muses as we reach the kitchen. My eyes widen when I see Landry has been busy in the minutes I've left her alone. She is now making pancakes and already has a plate full.

"Baby? What are you doing?" I ask as I reach her side.

"I wasn't sure if he'd want what we were having, so I figured I'd make pancakes," she states, as if it's clear as day.

"You didn't need to go to any trouble," Maverick tells her as he walks over to where my coffee pot is set up. He makes himself a cup then sits down at the table. "I'm Maverick," he says to Landry as we sit back down. She's carrying a huge-ass plate of pancakes which she places in the middle of the table. His eyes turn pure white for a minute when he grabs the plate, after a few seconds, they return to normal. He says not a damn word to me before he starts digging into his food. I know he's not saying anything because Landry is in the same room, but it irritates my panther and human self, nevertheless.

"Landry Welch. Paxton says you're a friend of his?" she asks.

"I am. We're both part of the Rogue Enforcers. So, Pax, tell me why you are in need of my help." Blunt as usual, there's no beating around the bush when it comes to my friend.

I explain everything that has happened so far,

including Esmerelda's unexpected arrival. "So, you see, I'll need your help to ensure the danger is eliminated." I fix myself some pancakes since they're right there and Landry grins at me as if to say, 'See, I knew you'd want some too!' I give her a wink but continue slathering them with butter and syrup.

Before he can answer, Esmerelda walks through the back door, a small bag hanging off her arm. Maverick makes a slight hissing sound and Esmerelda waves him off. He doesn't seem to intimidate her and I'm now thinking that this is going to be an interesting few days. "No, don't get up, I'm capable of getting my own coffee," she says to Landry. "This is for you," she states, handing the bag to Landry. "You can slip it in your pocket, but it's important that you keep it on you at all times." Maverick's and my nose both scrunch up trying to smell whatever it is that she gave her. Nothing, it's got no foreboding scent which eases my nerves a fraction. It's good to know Esmerelda has no intention of poisoning my mate. I'd hate to have to take the woman out since she has a connection to Landry's past, but I would in a heartbeat if she posed any threats.

"What is it?" Landry questions, looking at the bag. Thanks to the panther in me, I can smell the various herbs inside and wonder what the combination she has put together is supposed to do. Maverick's eyebrow raises, and he gives a slight nod which lets me know that he's picked up on the ingredients and is in agreement that it poses no danger. At least not to Landry.

Be careful, panther, it's dangerous to your kind if it's used on you in the wrong way, Maverick warns me through our link.

Not for him or Landry. The damn witch invades our inner conversation. Well fuck me, this answers so many things where it comes to this new person in our lives.

"It's designed to confuse anyone looking for you," Esmerelda explains as she fills up a plate with pancakes and fruit. "I'm glad you made these; I've been in the mood for pancakes."

If she's in danger, she can throw some of the powder at them and it will disable them as well, Esmerelda says through Maverick's and my shared link. But the information she just said is helpful.

"I heard that," Landry says out of thin air, causing all of us to whip our heads around and stare at her. "What? Isn't that a panther thing? That I can hear thoughts?" She shrugs her shoulders and I bite my lips to keep from laughing. Maverick and Esmerelda, however, have no such issues and bark out their own laughter.

Like I've said...life just got interesting and I can't wait to see how the ride of life works out with my mate who's full of surprises.

I agree, especially since she's the future mother to our cubs.

Fucker.

Landry

My life has definitely become off-kilter. I feel like I fell into an episode of *Outer Limits* or am riding the tilt-a-whirl at the amusement park. Ever since I woke up in Paxton's bed, the hits just keep on coming. First, I get told I'm a shifter, only to figure out after being bitten that I've always been one, she-bitch was just suppressed. Then, a witch shows up! I mean, Esmerelda seems like a good one, but how the hell would I know that? I've known a lot of people in my time who have fooled me. Now, there's another man sitting at the table and I can sense that he's something *other*-worldly as well, but I have no fucking clue what that could possibly be. Oh, and let's not forget the fact that now I can hear what Paxton, as well as the others, are thinking? Jesus fucking Christ. I just can't even right now. As much as I care about Paxton already, I almost wish I had never come here. Hell, this whole thing is as crazy as some of the books I've read. "Landry, what's going on in your head right now?" Esmerelda asks. I know she knows because she was responding to us yesterday based on our thoughts. I just think she wants me to verbally spew out all I'm feeling but it's all so jumbled, I know I'd look like an idiot.

"More than I can possibly express," I admit. "I just want to go back to bed and pull the covers over my head." Maybe even on my life...yeah, that'd be a good way to get out of this nightmare known as my life.

They're both here to help us. Don't be a pussy now.

But that's what we are puddy cat.

Oh, joy, you've got jokes today. I roll my eyes at her. I'm a hysterical bitch, thank you very much.

Great, now Queen Snarky is making sure to add her two fucking cents! Like I even asked her for her input...shit, I don't have to and she has a say about every little thing I do and think. She needs an off button. *All* of my life, I've felt so shitty about myself. I'm sure a psychologist would say it has to do with being abandoned as an infant, but a lot of it has to do with the orphanage I grew up in. I was apparently a sickly baby, so getting adopted was never a choice for me. I learned early on not to get attached to anyone, because they always left me. I also learned the hard way that not everyone who smiles at me is my friend. My so-called best friend, Aisha, was especially cruel when we got to middle school. I met her in third grade, and we became steadfast friends, but when we made it into the sixth grade, suddenly, she was so much better than I was. She spread vicious rumors about me leading up to several of the cute boys in our class jumping on board. Soon everyone was hopping aboard the lying train, saying I was nothing but a white-trash tramp. After that debacle, I spent my remaining school years behind the scenes. I also did as much as possible online to avoid being around my tormentors. I have no self-worth or self-confidence. So, it surprises me that I accepted Paxton into my life as readily as I did. I'm beginning to wonder, however, if it's due to the mate thing, or if it was an instant attraction...physical attraction. How would I know though? I was passed the hell out upon our first meeting.

I wanted to scratch all of them. A bunch of petty little bitches if you ask me. None of them could hold a candle to us. We were all that and a bag of chips.

Well, I didn't ask but I grin at her words, knowing that if she hadn't been bound, she would have shown herself and taken care of my bullies. I feel Esmerelda's hand on my arm and turn to look at her. "I wish that part could have been different for you," she murmurs. "I feel like I failed you in that aspect, but now that you've found your mate, the best is yet to come for you, Landry."

"If only," I whisper. "I-I just can't trust this, any of this, because everything I've ever wanted has been snatched away from me."

"Not this time. Never again," Paxton vows, picking me up and then sitting down with me in his lap. "You'll never be alone again, baby. And Maverick and Esmerelda are going to help me make sure that you're safe." His words are strong, but my past still is nagging me like a pesky little fly in the back of my mind. One day, I will beat the demons of my past and face a future as bright as the sun breaking through the clouds.

Home. We're finally home. Her purrs are loud and insistent as she rubs up against my insides. *Believe in him and his words and we'll never feel let down by life again. Trust, Landry. Just try to trust those who love us.*

I have to agree with her assessment because I've never felt as safe and secure as I do since Paxton came into my life, I just have to give it some more time before I'm fully confident of his words. I've learned that actions speak more than words and so far, his have been consistent.

He'll show you that he means what he says. We're safe now. Well, mostly. But he will protect us with his very life.

"So, what's the plan?" I ask, anxious to put the danger behind us so we can live without fear looming over us.

"Well, I want your permission to access your memories," Maverick states. He's still eating, and I momentarily wonder where he's putting all the food he's consumed.

"He's got a high metabolism, like all shifters," Esmerelda says.

"Gah, you too? It's not bad enough I have Queen Snarky privy to every thought but now I have you as well," I grumble. "I can see that my days of privacy are over. Done. Finished." Okay, I'm being dramatic but dammit all, I think I deserve to be able to throw a small hissy fit at least. Wait, Maverick wants to access my memories? What the hell? "What do you mean, access my memories?" I inquire, staring at Maverick.

"Ah, that's one of my abilities. Did Paxton tell you anything about me?" he asks.

"Not really, just that you were coming here to help us," I admit. "Which, by the way, I greatly appreciate."

"Well, you obviously now know there are shifters living among the humans," he says.

"Witches too, apparently, but superheroes aren't real," I reply.

Shut up and listen! This is important.

"No, they're not. Anyhow, I'm what's known as a hybrid." He sets his fork down and looks me square in the eyes, waiting to see how I'm going to handle this news.

I feel the world spin on its axis once again at his words. "What in the hell is a hybrid?" It can't be any worse than my imagination...right?

"I'm half wolf and half vampire." I find myself pulling back from him and cuddling closer to Paxton. When Maverick notices, he grins, and I see his canines elongate slightly. When I do a full-body shiver, he chuckles at my fear induced by his long, scary fangs that could rip my damn throat out.

"Stop scaring her, Mav!" Paxton growls out. And yeah, it's a growl; his panther is very near the surface.

"Sorry, sorry. I'm teasing you. While blood is one thing I need for nourishment, you're safe around me. I've never killed anyone by drinking blood...not on purpose anyway." He chuckles at his own sense of humor, but all I wanna do is get a cross and find the closest church. "Anyhow, I have the ability to enter your mind and search for memories. I'll be looking for anything that you might not remember that could help us with this...situation." My hand comes up to my throat and I wrap it securely around my neck. This causes the other three in the room to chuckle.

"Wait a second, you're out during the day. How?" I am genuinely curious now because I always thought if there were vampires, they couldn't be out in daylight.

"Myth. It's all a myth that humans came up with to make us scarier to the human race. I can be around garlic, crosses don't scare me, and I can walk through the doors of a church just like you can."

Fuck, there's nowhere for me to hide then. I wonder about holy water? The look he gives me lets me know that it doesn't bother him any more than the other stuff he previously mentioned. "Does it hurt?" I ask, jumping back to him searching my memories.

"Not from what I understand, no one has expressed being in any pain to me. It's more like a tickle and it won't take very long." He better be telling me the truth, otherwise his balls won't be safe from my knee. I may not be able to holy water him to death, but I can make him hurt.

I sigh, hating that he'll see some of the hell I've

gone through, but wanting to help in any way possible. "If you really think it'll help, then I'll do it. Can...can Paxton stay with me?"

"You can stay just as you are," Maverick says. He moves his chair so he's in front of us, then places his hands on either side of my head. "Okay, open your mind for me, Landry," he says, his voice dropping to a level that mesmerizes me. "Close your eyes and take a deep breath. Let all thoughts leave your mind and find a black hole and lay inside of it." I feel something, like a tickle, run through my head and giggle.

"Sorry, I'm ticklish," I murmur.

"Shh, it's okay. You were a beautiful shifter baby, Landry. You're your own brand of hybrid you know...half human and half panther, fascinating. Esmerelda, you haven't changed a bit, have you? Landry, you look just like your mother." His words wash over me, filling me with a warmth that I didn't know was missing. I hear him hiss in a breath and figure that he's now seeing the hell I lived during my school years. "You didn't deserve any of that sort of treatment," he mutters. "Or for that to happen either. For fuck's sake, what is wrong with people?" I feel the wetness sliding down my cheeks as my deepest shame is revealed, at least to him. Paxton's arms tighten around me and as his scent envelopes me, I relax once again. "You've never done a thing in your life to feel shame for. Other people's insecurities and bullying ways is on them, never you." Maverick's voice remains low and almost hypnotic as he states various things he's seeing.

"I've got you, baby," Paxton whispers in my ear. "Just a few minutes longer." I end up falling into a deep sleep while resting in Paxton's arms.

Chapter 10

Paxton

"Did you put her to sleep, Mav?" I question him as her dead weight causes her to lay limp in my arms.

"Figured it'd be easier for her to not dwell on the things of her past that she can't change. She'll wake up and the pain will be dulled. She needs to trust, and with all of that rambling around in her head, there's no way she'll open up and let any of us in."

"Her life's been hell, hasn't it?" I ask. I can feel my panther roaming restlessly and know he's feeling the heartbreak that I am over all that Landry has endured.

Must kill her tormentors.

"More than you know," he replies. He still has his hands on her head and I occasionally see his eyes flash white and then red, so I know her life has been shit. "Jesus fucking Christ," he hisses. "How in the *fuck* did she survive this hell?" he mutters. He's not giving me anything, but my mind automatically thinks the worst as all types of scenarios play out like a movie trailer on repeat.

"Do I need to kill anyone?" I question. He gives me a look but shakes his head.

"No, but it's only because she managed to get herself away before any real damage was done to her. However, the people involved were people she trusted, unconditionally, which is something she no longer allows to happen in her life. Looks like after all the betrayals she's suffered from those she did allow access to her heart, that's when she became distrustful of most people. *Fuck!*" He hisses again, and his eyes go white for so long I begin to wonder if I need to interfere somehow.

We will fix this.

Yes, fucking right, we will. Even only knowing her for a few days, I can tell she's got a gentle soul and generous heart, she didn't deserve anything she was put through while growing up. Based on how Maverick is acting, I believe it's worse than he's saying and that pisses me off. I'm her mate so I need to know in order to fix things.

Trust Mav. He has your best interests at heart. But we will hurt those who have hurt our mate. I promise. I will not rest, sleep, or eat until she's been avenged.

"Paxton, you've got your work cut out for you. She's got some issues, some will be easily won, but some battles will take more time, patience and understanding. She's worth it, and you will come out the victor in the long run. Should be a bit easier since you're mated already, but she is so insecure about herself that any little thing might send her running. Don't let that happen, you two are much stronger together than separate. She's a brave soul, just needs some coaxing to get her through the triggers of the past."

"She's not leaving me, man," I tell him, unconsciously pulling my sleeping mate closer.

"She may not physically leave, but she can always check out emotionally. Throughout the years, she's gotten good at finding that place buried in her head and is able to escape there when things get too hard to deal with," he replies.

"We won't allow that to happen," Esmerelda interjects. While Maverick has been doing his thing, she's been hovering, not saying a word, but doing things with shit she pulled out of her bag. At one point, I noticed her with her hands near, but not touching, Maverick, and I swear I saw a purplish-blue glow surround him. A small part of me wonders why that was, but I realize that if they want me to know, they'll tell me. Both of them only have Landry's best interests at heart and while I don't know Esmerelda the way I know Maverick, she's been protecting my mate for all of her life, so I trust her to know what's best. At least I'm starting to lean that way, I need to spend more time with her before she has gained my utmost confidence in that area.

Mav sweeps his hands one more time across Landry's head and down along her jaw before he breathes in deeply and once again, she slumps into a deep slumber in my arms. I would worry that her eyes never opened, but Mav and Esmerelda seem to be at peace, so I don't ask any questions...yet. I take a good look at him and see how haggard he suddenly looks and realize just how much traipsing through Landry's memories has affected him. It takes a strain on him emotionally and physically every time he does this—uses this gift he's been given—but he never lets it stop him from helping others. Esmerelda also looks a bit puny and of course, I can't forget the sleeping beauty in my arms. "I think we all need to take a break, don't you?" I ask the two of them.

"I need to recharge again, yes," Esmerelda replies. "Young man, I have the room off to the right. See that you don't come in unless invited," she says to Maverick.

He raises his eyebrows and asks, "Why not?" His tone isn't his usual one; it's as if he's genuinely curious as to why he can't go into the room Esmerelda is using.

"Because I have some ongoing spells I'm working on and if you break the plane of my room, they'll dissipate, and that'll piss me off. Do you want to be turned into a bullfrog?"

"Only if you find me a princess to kiss me into a prince." His bark of laughter startles me but Landry sleeps on.

"You can do that?" I inquire. "How would that even work? A hairy frog with fangs?" Now the visual is in my head and I start to chuckle. Soon, Maverick is joining me which is highly unusual. I think my woman has worked some sort of magic on him because he's usually surly at the best of times.

"Never you mind how it works. Just stay away, please," Esmerelda states as she picks up her bag and prepares to head back to the tiny home.

"You need any help getting up?" Maverick asks me. "I can take her while you stand."

The growl that leaves my mouth has him taking a step back. "No, I've got it. Think my panther would go batshit crazy if you touched her again. He's already stressed the fuck out. Appreciate it though. Go get some rest and recharge."

"Sounds like a plan." It's plain as day that he's amused at my overabundance of protection of my mate. My panther and I are of like mind when we want to break the limb off of any part of the anatomy that touches what's ours.

"Maverick?" When he turns to look at me, I simply say, "Thank you."

"Not a problem, man. I got your back and now hers," he replies, waving his hand at Landry. "Guessing that was hard for you to say with your panther so close, huh?" He chuckles as he leaves me standing there with my mouth wide open.

"Funny son of a bitch. I can't wait until he finds his mate, I'm gonna give him so much grief he won't know which way he's turning," I mutter under my breath as I head in the direction of our bedroom.

It takes me a few minutes to get the two of us

situated in bed, but Landry never stirs. I pull her into my arms and breathe in her scent, hoping it will relax me. My job now is to find those who made her life a living hell and take care of them, but I need to wait until we resolve the threat from that alpha before I work on that, however, and it will happen.

Yes, it will. I saw, Paxton, and she was treated terribly. Some of the people in that orphanage would beat her up and hurt her. That cannot stand.

No, no it can't. As I lay there, willing myself to sleep for a bit, I realize that I need to talk to her about moving in since we're mates. We can't be apart for long periods of time and I'm established here. Hopefully, whatever she does for a living is mobile in nature so that she can still do it living here.

Good call, getting Maverick here. Our mate will be just fine.

My panther's words ringing in my ears, I begin to drift off to sleep.

Fuck yeah, she will.

Yes, she will, I hear Esmerelda say in my head.

Let me be witch.

Then, I have a laughing Maverick and it pisses me off to the point that I put a wall up on our link.

There, take that motherfuckers. Paxton has officially left the chat room.

Landry

I WAKE UP SURROUNDED BY WARMTH AND REALIZE THAT Paxton is snuggled up against me. I don't know when I fell asleep but the last thing I remember is Maverick telling me I didn't deserve the things that have happened to me. Recalling that has me taking a trip down memory lane only to find that the pain and hurt which has always been present is some-how...less than it was before. Funnily enough, I hear echoes of what sounds like Maverick's voice telling me to hold my head up, the best is yet to come. Weird, huh?

I try to wiggle away from Paxton only to hear, "Stop moving, baby, unless you plan to take care of what you've caused." I giggle when I realize he's hard against me and find myself pushing back just a tiny bit. "Woman, you don't realize how close you are to being thoroughly ravished," he bites out. I can hear a slight growl and it dawns on me that whatever he heard while Maverick was traipsing through my memories likely has him feeling stressed. Instead of replying, I roll over so we're face-to-face and cup his cheek in my hand.

"Paxton, it's probably too early, but life is too short, don't you think?" I murmur.

"Too early for what?" The confused look he has makes me smile and I lean forward just enough so our lips brush.

"To tell you how I feel." I bite my lip, suddenly unsure if I should speak my mind. But life is short, life has taught me that lesson and I'm not sure I like the thought that something could happen to one of us today and he'd never know how much my heart has opened up to him.

Tell mate that you love him. Do it now!

Hush up, you damn hussy! We've talked about interfering in each other's time. This is one of those, so back the fuck off. I shake my head at the fact that the sassy, saucy she-bitch is practically yelling at me as she paces inside.

"It's never too early for that," he replies, softly kissing me back.

"I love you. Maybe it's because we're mates, maybe it's because it was love at first sight. Don't know and don't care, just know that you're like air to me. I crave your presence, whether we're sleeping, eating, or making love. I want you near me."

His smile lights up his face before he replies, saying, "Part of it is likely the mating bond, but I think that what you feel, what *I* feel, will continue to grow stronger. Because I love you too."

I feel my heart start beating so fast that for a minute, I feel lightheaded. Never in my whole life has anyone said that they loved me and the feelings his words evoke in me have me in tears. "Y-y-you do?" I whisper. "Really?" I know there are now tears streaming down my face because he is blurry, but I still see his nod before his thumbs come up and start wiping my face.

"God, Landry, please don't cry, sweetheart. I've got you, I'll always have you."

"I'll do everything I can to be the best mate, Paxton. I'll make you proud and never shame you when we're in front of your friends."

"You could never shame me, Landry. You are bright, full of life and my friends will adore you. Mates are special, there's a unique bond that is treasured. You, my dear, are my gem, the most beautiful, valuable thing I have in my life. Nothing, and I mean nothing you do, would ever make me want to abandon you. You are stuck with me whether you like it or not."

Mate is very good with words.

Yes, yes, he is, and I can feel my desire ramp up.

When I see his eyes flare, I ask, "Think we have time to, you know, fool around a little bit?"

He winks at me before rolling until he's half on top of me. "We have all the time in the world, baby. In fact, we have a lifetime of loving ahead of us."

"Show me."

"It'll be my pleasure."

Chapter 11

Paxton

I leave Landry sleeping and head out to the back to see if Maverick wants to run the property with me. I normally wouldn't do it twice in one day, but I woke up after several hours of fun with Landry to a niggling sense that something wasn't right, and I need to check it out.

"Pax, I was coming to see if you wanted to check on things," Mav says as I approach him as he walks from the tiny house toward me. "Something's not right and the witch is inside chanting and shit, so I figure we need to see what's going on."

"Will Landry be okay? It takes roughly thirty

minutes to run my property and if Esmerelda is other-wise occupied, it leaves her vulnerable since she's still asleep." I can't help but worry about her every second I'm away from her. Between the current threat and the memories of the past, she's been a bit restless in sleep.

"She should be fine, but you have to remember, she's a shifter and will sense any danger." This should make me feel better, but seeing as she's only been a shifter for a few short days and is still getting used to her senses, the words don't do anything to ease my worries.

"Mav, she just found out she's a damn shifter, for fuck's sake! She won't know what to do." I'm feeling the stress, almost like a physical caress, and run my fingers through my hair. If I keep doing this, I may go bald which would likely piss my panther off since he cherishes his deep dark fur.

Bald is not allowed, mate would be highly displeased. Plus, how do I clean something that's non-existent? He really sounds annoyed and ready to brawl. It'll have to wait for later though, right now I have a property to canvass.

"Her panther will know what to do, Paxton. Instinct, remember? Plus, she has that thing that Esmerelda gave her. I saw her put it around her neck." I breathe a sigh of relief, remembering the small bag of herbs and whatever else Esmerelda tossed in the amulet that is hanging around my love's neck.

"Still doesn't keep my panther from being restless. Something's not right, Mav. I just can't seem to put my finger on what that is, and it has me tied up in knots."

"Then let's go check things out so we can get back," he replies, before quickly stripping and shifting. Somehow, he knows something, but dammit, he's not sharing and until he does, the best I can do is follow his lead and check my property again. Once I shift, we head off to run the property.

We get back after checking everything out and I calm down once I realize that if Maverick feels the course of someone's life will change, he won't share what he sees. He has visions, so it's possible that whatever he's seeing is what had me initially on edge because there was nothing, not one thing, that was out of place on my land.

"Good looking asses, you two," Esmerelda says as she walks out onto the porch of the tiny cabin while we're both redressing. I snarl at her, but she grins and states, "Hey, I know you're a taken man, but I can appreciate a well-formed ass."

"You shouldn't be looking," I state.

"Oh, honey, I'm a woman, I'll always look. I'm old, not dead," she snickers, and Mav's face has a look of someone who's been scorned.

"I...I have no words." Mav throws his hands up in defeat and marches into the house, clothes firmly clutched in his hand.

"Woohee, if I was a young gal, I'd go claim that man for my own." She starts fanning her face with her hands.

"You aren't that old," I murmur.

"Only in years and experience. Speaking of, maybe I should go give that boy some pointers for when he finds his mate. I'm pretty sure he could use a lesson here or there."

"Esmerelda? Never mind, I have no words." Just as stumped as Mav was of what to say, I turn my back and walk towards my cabin, my love, my mate. Hopefully Esmerelda hasn't worn off on my woman and I can find some sanity and sanctuary with my woman in my arms.

As soon as I cross over the threshold, I hear the water running in the bathroom and realize that Landry is now up and soaping up her body in the shower. I can get behind that; I get excited at the aspect of rubbing my hands up and down her skin. Grinning, I drop my clothes and go to join her, seeing as my run has left me sweaty. As far as excuses go, that's a damn good one if you ask me.

"About time you got here," she says as I step into the shower. It makes my heart warm at the thought that she's as desperate to be near me as I am where it concerns her.

"Did you miss me?" I ask, pulling her close and kissing her. I can already feel through our link the need she has for me to be close to her; but for some reason I long to hear the words.

"Maybe?" she teases as her hands begin to roam. I see how this shower is going to go, and despite the imminent threat looming over our heads, I'm all for taking a break, especially one as enjoyable as the one we're going to have.

Landry

THIS GLORIOUS, SEXY MAN OF MINE IS GOING TO eventually be the death of me! Right now, he's passed out in our bed, so I decide to get dressed, then I head into the kitchen to see what I can rummage up and put together, for us to eat.

Mate is insatiable. I couldn't agree with her more on this topic.

Ya think? I'm ridiculously glad for the increased stamina that I have because if I were a mere mortal, as I always believed I was, I wouldn't be walking, of that I'm confident. I see Esmerelda sitting at the kitchen table drinking a cup of tea and roll my eyes. Apparently, she prefers our kitchen to the one in the tiny house, even though it has everything necessary. "Child, the two of you need to focus," she says, taking another sip of tea. "We've got to get this resolved."

I raise a brow at her as I open the fridge. "I thought you were working some of your magic to figure out where the alpha was located. Can't do anything until that part is done, right?" Spying the hash brown casserole I knew was there, I grab that, my mouth salivating while anticipating the glorious taste soon to hit my tongue and heat it up in the microwave. With all the sex I've been having, my metabolism is running even higher than what I'd perceive as normal, and despite eating, I've lost weight. I'm loving my lithe, muscular new body. There are some perks I'm finding marvelous to having a panther residing within me after all; I finally found the silver-lining.

Now if you'd only agree to the hairy legs.

"Correct. I also wanted to bring you something,"

she says, opening up her bag and pulling out a small package. I'm starting to worry with all the powders and potions she's been handing me lately to keep on my person. I'm not used to all of this drama that seems to be surrounding me since I was injured.

"What is it?" I question, as I head to the table with my food bounty in hand.

"Take a look at it," she invites, waving her hand. I put my plate down and slowly take the package from her as she hands it over. Hmm, not too heavy, not too light. I shake it and don't hear any rattling. This doesn't exactly feel like Christmas morning, but I do love receiving presents since it wasn't something I'm used to be given freely. "For the love of the goddesses, open the damn thing," Esmerelda snaps. I have to bite down the growl that the she-bitch wants to let loose.

I roll my eyes and slowly open the box. Inside is a photo album and instinctively, I know it holds pictures of my mother. My heart clenching, I slowly, reverently, open the picture book. Tears spring to my eyes when the first page enters my vision; it's of whom I'm presuming is my mom, seeing as I'm her doppelgänger and all, she's holding me in her arms tightly. But it's the look of happiness on her face that has me captivated. Pure, unadulterated, unwavering joy almost radiates from the picture. I glance over at Esmerelda through misty eyes and see hers look wet as well. I continue flipping through the album and am amazed that there are so many, considering from what Esmerelda said, neither of my parents lived very long after I was born. There are even pictures with the three of us—me, my mom and my dad; and those are labeled. "I-I look like her," I finally manage to say through my sobs.

"You have your father's eye color and his temperament, but other than that, you two could have been twins," she replies. "They were good to you, despite the brevity of their involvement in your life, Landry. They loved you so very much. I just wish I had been able to get there sooner with some of my friends; perhaps, the outcome would've been different."

"It wouldn't have changed a thing," Maverick states, walking into the kitchen. "This—what happened to her parents; had to happen. It's the way destiny meant for it to play out. It had to happen this way, in order for the rest of what's to come to happen as it was designed by the council, our higher powers." Ah, and there's our vague-speaking houseguest.

"Well, now that the gang's all here, can we find the alpha and get this shit done? I've got a life to live, folks, and this is putting a crimp in what I've got going on." I hear a knock on the front door and start to head in that direction when I *feel* Paxton telling me not to move. I shake my head because I *heard* him, but I know he didn't speak out loud. Before I can say anything, he appears and gives a slight nod of his head to Maverick, who moves around me so that the two of them can head to the front door.

Chapter 12

Paxton

Maverick and I both know that my house is secluded, and it's very rare for visitors to make their way to my front door, unless specifically invited by me. The fact that I heard no cars making their way up the drive has the hairs on the back of my neck standing on end.

I open the door, Mav at my side, and step out onto the porch. The slimy fucker on my porch has my hackles rising, even if he hasn't said a damn word. "Who the fuck are you?" I intently question. I can feel my panther right at the surface and know it won't take much for him to make himself known.

"I've come here to take ownership of what is mine," the unknown male says. "Your property is surrounded, so let's make it easy on everyone. Hand her over and no one will get hurt." I sniff the air, and sure enough, I can smell the atrocious smell of infected shifters, what they're addicted to is a familiar scent, but I can't seem to place it because of the fury running through me. My ears are pounding and my claws are extended...it's a protective instinct to be partially shifted so it won't take long for me to complete the shift if the need shall arise.

Mate isn't going anywhere!

You've got that right. I feel Maverick move closer as he replies, "You sure about that? Not everything is evident to the naked eye." When I glance at him, the bastard winks at me and gives me a slight nod and I realize that somehow, he's called in reinforcements. Without telling me, I might add, but I appreciate it and am enamored at the precautions he's taken on my mate's behalf. The only thing that matters and is of utmost importance is keeping Landry safe.

"What are you talking about, half-breed?" the apparent leader snarls at Maverick. I hear Maverick chuckle; the sound is chilling, and I have to steel myself against taking a step back from him. Glancing at the three men on my porch, I see their eyes widen and know that Maverick has partially shifted, which is a sight in and of itself. He's basically a wolf on steroids who also happens to have a set of fangs that could rip your throat out.

"This has been foretold; you're merely a pawn in this game," Maverick replies. Granted, it's growled out, but the words are clear enough that two of the men step back from their leader. They look lost and confused, it's odd and nothing I've ever witnessed before from others.

"Alpha, you said this wouldn't be any issue," dumbass one states. He's still looking at the alpha with hero worship in his eyes and you can tell he's willing to do whatever is commanded of him.

"It isn't an issue. They just need to hand the woman over to us," the man who I now know is the alpha replies. "Give her to me. Now." Does this piece of shit actually think he's gonna give me orders and I'm gonna do his bidding? What a crock of shit, she will leave with him over my dead body.

"Not happening, motherfucker. She's my mate and I'm not letting her go," I snarl.

We can kill him.

I'm down with that, I reply to him.

I'm most certainly onboard with my panther's plans and thoughts where it comes to this wanna-be standing in front of me issuing orders. My panther and I are about to take the offensive pose and do just that when I hear Esmerelda. *If you cut off the head of the snake, the body will scatter and die.*

What the fuck? I wonder if perhaps she has lost her mind when Maverick chimes in as well. *We kill the alpha and the others will go.* Huh. I'm about to reply once again, it's beginning to feel like a game, when Landry presses against my back and peers around me. Before I have the opportunity to do anything, I witness her hand come around me and a powder-like substance flies into the eyes of the three men on my porch.

"What the fuck?" dumbass one yells, rubbing at his eyes. "What did you do to us?" They begin sneezing in a rhythm that nearly has me forgetting what's taking place and laughing at their predicament.

I remember the powder that Esmerelda gave her in the bag, as well as Maverick's warning to me that if used improperly, it can cause harm to panthers. Moving toward the men, I grab the alpha by the collar of his shirt and drag him away from the others. "Paxton? It's him, isn't it?" Landry questions, pointing to the alpha.

"Yeah, baby, it is," I tell her. I hear a snarl and see buttons fly, then watch as her panther skirts around me. Before I can personally act and do anything where the slimeball is concerned, she reaches up and swipes across the alpha's face before she turns to dumbass one. Fuck, my mate is a badass.

That turned me on. Me too, buddy, me too.

"Get her off me," dumbass one screams. With Landry now occupied, Maverick and I make quick work of completely disabling the alpha.

Cut off the head, insists Esmerelda, invading my thoughts again. *She'll never be safe again if you don't.*

I sit on our porch, shirtless as is Mav after shifting and assisting my mate in taking down a few motherfuckers. Maverick and Esmerelda are sitting close by in the other two chairs that occupy my front porch as we keep our eyes glued so we can keep a close watch on Landry as she continues to lick the dripping, wet blood from her paws. Meanwhile, the men that were with the alpha, as well as others who Maverick's contacts rounded up, are wandering around my front yard, dazed and confused as fuck.

"What do you think happened to them?" I ask, pointing my beer out at the men stumbling around. Landry roars at my question, that's one pissed off panther she's harboring, then as if nothing happened, she goes back to cleaning herself.

"Their alpha imbued them with his blood so that they would listen without question and obey his every command," Esmerelda states. She's sipping wine out of a wine glass, one that I had no clue I even owned. It probably came from that damn bag she carries, but right now, I couldn't care less. "Yes, I bring my own glass since not everyone is sophisticated enough to own wine glasses. I do like my creature comforts." Why does she insist on speaking like someone who's not of our time? Drives me freaking insane!

I hate when she does that!

Pot meet kettle. Damn nosy fucker keeps wanting to intervene whenever Landry and I are being intimate.

I could shift, and she and I could have some fun.

No, no, no! She's had a rather busy day, plus we need to get rid of all these people on my property. I am not happy about them all being here while you frolic and play with our mate, not in the least. Maverick's other 'friends' are slowly rounding them up, but it's taking too fucking long as far as I'm concerned. "Landry, baby, you wanna go in and get a shower?" I ask, anxious to reconnect with her. I watch as her head turns toward me, and she blinks slowly before standing on all four legs and walking toward the front door. "You got this?" I ask Esmerelda and Maverick, only to see her wave her hand almost imperiously and him nod in confirmation. By the time I reach the door itself, I can hear Landry purring. Even though she's obviously not ready to shift back to her human form, I still need my hands on her at least so I lead us to our bathroom. Once the water is perfect, I motion for her to get inside and then proceed to lather her up and bathe her. Who knew that tearing someone limb from limb could be so damn gory? I mean, I know that because it's happened to me, but I sure as hell never expected to watch my mate do that very thing.

Mate was fucking awesome.

I nod as I double check her paws to make sure she didn't harm herself and smile when she rubs her head against my arm. "Love you, Landry. You're safe now," I murmur. "I guess we need to get the rest of your things moved here." I know she can't answer right now, but she can understand me and will respond when she shifts.

Landry

I wake up warm and dry, in human form, curled into Paxton's arms. As the memories of the morning flood my mind, I cringe and wonder how he's going to feel after seeing me destroy someone. Well, several someones actually. "You're thinking too fucking hard, woman," he rasps out, kissing me behind my ear. "You were fucking awesome earlier, a total badass. Both Mav and I were impressed at how you held your own."

"You two helped me," I state, rolling so that we're facing one another. I don't remember much after anger took me over and I allowed my panther to be in control. She wanted vengeance, and I wasn't going to stand in the way of her getting her pound of flesh.

"We did, baby. Not because we didn't think you could handle it, but because neither of us like a lot of people around and wanted it finished up."

"Well, I'm happy my she-bitch was willing to share that privilege with you two, she was sorta snarky and insisting on taking over. I decided she was better equipped to handle the situation than I was...so I let her."

Paws with claws trumps toes with nails.

"Queen Snarky is funny today. But you said something earlier about picking up the rest of my stuff," I say. He smiles at me, and my knees quiver in need. Down kitty, we have a lifetime left to love on our man.

This time, I'm not speaking to my panther, but my inner self who wants to rub all over her man.

"Yeah, since we're mates and you're living with me now, we need to get the rest of your things moved in." Hmmm...wonder how he's about to take the news I'm fixing to share with him?

"You already got all my stuff, Paxton," I whisper. "Since I'm a professional athlete with sponsors and I travel all over, I don't have an actual home. The two suitcases you picked up from my hotel are all I own." I feel his arms tighten around me at my words.

"You're home, Landry," he says.

Finally, I have a home, one where I'm loved and where there'll be laughter for the rest of my days. "Think we can celebrate that fact?"

I agree with this plan.

Shut it, Queen Snarky, I'm about to get busy with my man.

Epilogue

Paxton

Three Months Later

I know Landry has been dying for us to shift together and roam the property. Today's that day. The weather is perfect, not that it would matter all that much, and after a hearty breakfast, we shift and head out to explore our land. Now that I've taught her more about our ways, we often spend our time talking without uttering a word, and today is no different.

'*Can we stay out all day?*' she asks.

'*We can stay out as long as you'd like,*' I reply, watching her sashay in front of me.

'*What plans are you cooking up?*'

'Planning on having my way with you at some point,' I admit. At my words, she strikes a pose before running away from me.

'You've got to catch me first, Paxton,' she hollers. Not wanting to be outdone, I give chase.

Best fucking day of my life.

I THINK WE MADE CUBS TODAY.

I roll my eyes as I cover my woman back up. She's sound asleep and I have to admit, my ego is puffed out because she dozed off within minutes of coming. It might have something to do with our earlier escapades down by the stream when we were still in our panther form, but I'd prefer to believe that I wore her out.

I'm positive we made cubs. Can you smell it?

Oh Jesus. Knowing he isn't going to relent, I breathe in deeply and catch the faint difference in her scent. Could...could my panther be correct? I know humans wouldn't know so quickly, but he's been such a pain in the ass about adding cubs that if there's any way for him to know this early, he would.

Yes, I can tell the difference. She's going to have my cubs.

"Just saying, they'll be ours, not just yours," I whisper. Landry's so out of it, she doesn't even stir. Of course, because both of our panthers seem to have their own personalities, it's not unusual for either of us to be caught talking out loud.

Whatever. I knew first.

I drift off to sleep realizing that life as I know it is once again about to change. I went from a surly loner who thought he would be alone the rest of his life, to a mated man. Granted, my mate comes with a witch as a godmother, but I have my friends as well, so it probably makes us even. I honestly can't wait to see what the future holds—with the two of us, for the Rogue Enforcers, and as future parents.

The End

Coming Soon To The Rogue Enforcers Series

Releasing November 2019

Alarik

By Tracie Douglas

Stay tuned for more book by other amazing authors in this shared world.
Rogue Enforcers Lineup:

Colton: Rogue Beginnings
By Grace Brennan
US: My Book
Maxwell
By Livell James
US: My Book
Marcel
By Rennie Rivera
US: My Book
Rhys
By Theresa Hissong
US: https://amzn.to/2nU2eGW

Paxton

Coming Soon
November 2019 - Tracie Douglas

December 2019 - Desiree Lafawn

January 2020 - Liberty Parker

February 2020 - Samantha McCoy

To keep up to date on all the news, cover reveals, and releases from the Rogue Enforcer Series, join the Facebook group!

www.facebook.com/
groups/RogueEnforcersreadergroup

Acknowledgments

Special thanks to Grace Brennan for opening up her paranormal world, not only to me, but to the other ten authors who have joined in this fantastical adventure. Each of our stories are unique with the running theme being that these shifters are ones who, for whatever reason, were not good candidates for the actual Enforcers!

I'm a lifelong reader who had a dream to write her own books. A transplanted Yankee, I recently moved cross country from Georgia to Texas. While I have a strong personal belief system and faith, I won't be "preaching" in any of my books. They'll have perfectly imperfect people in it who meet, fall in love, fall into bed (at times; sometimes they might wait), have kids, get married. In short, I want to write books that make people think and feel.

My debut novel, "Bountiful Harvest" was released on the 7th anniversary of my mom's death. Somehow, I think my biggest cheerleader and staunchest defender helped it publish so quickly.

Since hitting publish 8/31/16, I've had the privilege to begin co-writing with Liberty Parker on an MC series, the Rebel Guardians. There are seven books out in this series, plus two books in a spin-off (2.0, the next generation) and the first book in The Nelson Brothers (who show up in book 5 of the RGMC). We're hard at work on yet another spin-off (New Beginnings) featuring some of the girls from the RGMC whose love interests are not with the men from the MC!

I also co-write a series of children's short stories with a fellow author, Cherry Shephard and her 10 year old son. Get immersed in "The Mischief Kitties" and their zany, crazy lives!

facebook.com/darlenetallmanauthor
bookbub.com/authors/darlene-tallman

<u>Standalones</u>

<u>Bountiful Harvest</u>

<u>His Firefly</u>

<u>His Christmas Pixie</u>

<u>Her Kinsman-Redeemer</u>

<u>Operation Valentine</u>

<u>His Forever</u>

<u>Forgiveness</u>

<u>Christmas With Dixie</u>

<u>Our Last First Kiss</u>

<u>Draegon: The Falder Clan - Book One</u>

<u>Scars of the Soul</u>

<u>Hale's Song</u>

<u>The Mischief Kitties (with Cherry Shephard)</u>

<u>The Mischief Kitties in Bampires & Ghosts & New Friends, Oh My!</u>

The Mischief Kitties in the Great Glitter Caper

The Mischief Kitties in You Can't Takes Our Chicken

Black Tuxedos

The Black Tuxedos MC

1. The Black Tuxedos MC - Reese

2. Nick - The Black Tuxedos MC

Rebel Guardians MC (with Liberty Parker)

Braxton

Hatchet

Chief

Smokey & Bandit

Law

Capone

A Twisted Kind Of Love

Rebel Guardians Next Generation (with Liberty Parker)

1. Talon & Claree

2. Jaxson & Ralynn

New Beginnings (with Liberty Parker)

1. Reclaiming Maysen

2. Reviving Luca

Nelson Brothers (with Liberty Parker)

1. Seeking Our Revenge

2. Seeking Our Forever

Old Ladies Club (with Kayce Kyle, Erin Osborne and Liberty Parker)

1. Old Ladies Club - Wild Kings MC

2. The Old Ladies Club - Soul Shifterz MC

3. Old Ladies Club - Rebel Guardians MC

4. Old Ladies Club - Rage Ryders MC

With Various Other Authors

Poetry: Dreams You Catch

www.ingramcontent.com/pod-product-compliance
Lightning Source LLC
Chambersburg PA
CBHW071951150726

47999CB00001B/396